WILD SPACE SAGA BOOK 1

BETWEEN
THE
DEVIL
AND THE
DARK

WILD SPACE SAGA BOOK 1

BETWEEN THE DEVIL AND THE DARK

BRANDON HILL &
TERENCE PEGASUS

4 Horsemen
Publications, Inc.

4 Horsemen
Publications, Inc.

4 Horsemen Publications, Inc.
1497 Main St. Suite 169
Dunedin, FL 34698
4horsemenpublications.com
info@4horsemenpublications.com

Cover by Jenn K
Typesetting by Niki Tantillo.
Editor: Laura Mita

Library of Congress Control Number: 2022932694

Paperback ISBN-13: 978-1-64450-570-0
Hardcover ISBN-13: 978-1-64450-638-7
Audiobook ISBN-13: 978-1-64450-568-7
Ebook ISBN-13: 978-1-64450-569-4

DEDICATION

Special thanks to our Patrons, Louise Burge, Paul Lucas, and D. Banks for your support, and to 4 Horsemen Publications for believing in us!

And a big thanks to our DeviantArt and IRL followers. You're what keeps us going! Keep following the Northwest Passage with us!

Hana IV

MAELSTROM
NEBULA

Holsk

Haven

Mandela I

Siberna

Dorado

Sepra

Zade

Halo
Meridian

Columbus

Zynj

COLONIAL
ALLIANCE

Beauvior
III

Bartholomew VII

TABLE OF CONTENTS

PROLOGUE

Agent Four kept his poker-faced decorum as he stepped up to the communication room's dais. He waited for the biometric scans to finish, giving his spotless black suit an unnecessary dust off.

Four could sense that the universe was changing. Stealing a glance out of the ship's observation deck on his way, he noticed the undeniable signs: the increasing number of capital ships and platoons of soldiers filling the Imperial barracks and garrisons. War was coming, and this was only the tip of a massive iceberg, one that went back at least two decades.

Two decades of decisions that became ever more extreme.

Of course, there was little that he, much less Nemesis, could do about it. Both he and the one he cared for were mere cogs in the Imperial machine, expendable at a moment's whim—a fact that took him years to discover, and even longer to accept.

In a moment, the hologram before him changed. A blank void featuring the words, DECODING INTERSTELLAR RELAY SIGNAL TO ICONA. PLEASE WAIT, switched to the face of Agent Two. Behind his superior, a red-orange sunset silhouetted Icona's ocean of skyscrapers and towering arcologies that composed the capital of Bistran.

"You've been activated." His words, direct and curt, were as inflectionless as his appearance was bland and nondescript: a trait of the Agents. Aside from his more slender build and longer brown hair, he wore the same black three-piece suit and glasses as Four. "Siberna Prime. Infiltration and retrieval of assets."

"Who's the mark?" Four asked.

The hologram of a young man appeared adjacent to the image of Two: a person of medium build, wearing a blue aviator's jacket over a blue-gray turtleneck and dark blue jeans and worn-looking black military boots. His face had a slightly narrow but squared jawline, large, mischievous-looking eyes that were a darker shade of green than his own, and a thick crown of black hair that seemed to be in a perpetual state of being blown away. His wide mouth was set in a grin that hinted at a sense of cockiness. Below, a straight line of a beard led to his chin, where it fanned out into a dark, sparse stubble. Beneath his left eye was a tattoo of two vertical parallelograms connected at the top by a diagonal line, the left one longer and set lower than the right.

"A pirate?" Four remarked, immediately recognizing the tattoo pattern. He narrowed his eyes, unseen by Agent Two behind their shades.

"Not just any pirate." Two shook his head. "He is Xerxes Paraska, the maternal first cousin of Pirate King Iriid."

"What's he doing on Siberna?"

"Working as a Gestalt Pilot, for the GI Leagues," Two replied. "Intelligence says he's grown quite a reputation for himself."

After hearing the ping of a finished download, Four skimmed over the information that appeared on the console in front of him. "Five-time ranking in the GI finals ... two-time champion ... Happily married to a Mandelan refugee ... crewmembers: human and itinerant Felyan techies ... He's high profile. Won't he be missed?"

"That's why you've been chosen for the retrieval—" The ghost of a smile appeared at the edge of his thin lips, "—both you and your partner, that is. I'm confident that you'll figure out how to handle it."

After a moment's gamble with his better judgment, Four at last decided to ask the question that had been standing at the edge of his lips.

"Exactly why do you need him?"

After seeing his superior's raised eyebrow, he quickly added, "If you don't mind my asking. After all, his being so popular is bound to make for some difficulties. You can't blame my curiosity."

"Political destabilization," Two answered after a somewhat lengthy silence of his own. With an unreadable frown, he seemed to study something off-screen before speaking again. "The 'Clans of the Free Trade Conglomerate,' as the King has grown to call his little kingdom, is becoming too powerful and prying too much into Imperial affairs. And projections state that renewing efforts to locate Rhoma and King's Knight might cost us a decade or longer than last expected. All the while, searching for their homeworlds, we'd be wasting time on increasing police actions against pirate raids—a costly enough venture in the long run. This way spares us time and money and gains us political leverage."

Two's ensuing silence was abrupt and poignant, and Four inferred that this was all the information he was going to get. It was a good thing, then, that he was good at doing a great deal with very little.

"Understood, sir," he said.

"One last thing," Two said before terminating the call. "The mission has a secondary, conditional mandate: retrieval or destruction of the asset." There was another pregnant pause. "Retrieval, however, is preferable."

"Understood, sir," Four replied again, and the hologram vanished, leaving him with the image of his target, mission data, and his thoughts.

And he began to think in earnest.

ONE

PLANET SIBERNA: SIBERNA PRIME: PIT TOWN DISTRICT

"**D**id we have to have the rest of the crew in orbit?" Xerx groaned into the comm at his wrist. He had forgotten how tedious, not to mention uncomfortable, maintenance work could be. Years ago, he would have felt at home perched on the shoulder of any Gestalt, but now, every ache reminded him of how acutely out of practice he was. And in spite of the harness, he began to develop an increasingly nauseating awareness of the sheer fifty-meter drop to the hangar floor.

He heard Neela's musical laugh at his complaint, her console at the hangar's far end hidden from sight by *Imani*'s massive form.

"You were the one who was so eager to get the *Reckless*' main engines online, *kipenzi*," his wife reminded him. And all things considered, it was a good decision. He'd just brought the ancient First Imperium warship out of storage on the far side of Siberna's greater moon a month ago, and it had only undergone a handful of shakedown runs.

"I thought we'd have some 'us' time," Xerx replied as he clambered up the hill-like, lobstered steel plates of *Imani*'s right shoulder, using the hoist's control wand to take out the slack from the harness and hasten his movements. "After all, when was the last time we got away from the rest of the crew? Last year?"

"Such are the sacrifices of a champion," Neela answered. "But for the romantic thought, I'll blow you a kiss... ah! It doesn't go that far."

Xerx sighed loudly. "Yeah, I didn't think this one through, I guess. I thought this job would go a lot faster than it's been ... oof!" He yanked at a lifted seam on an armor plate, but it wouldn't budge. Pressing his feet against an adjacent purchase, he pulled with all his strength. Slowly, it slid the rest of the way with an echoing groan. Xerx tapped into his control pad and after diverting the power feed, de-polarized the mass of nanogel that locked the wiring in place. He then moved the blue-gray rectangular paneling to the side, holding it in place with a magnetic bolt before he went to probing the mass of cables that protruded from the exposed muscle fibers. A series of green lights blinked on his pad, indicating a high-bandwidth datalink with Neela's console. "Ah, now we're in business," Xerx said with a note of satisfaction.

Neela's voice sounded much less sanguine. "Have you even worked as a climber before?"

Xerx snorted. "I've worked with plenty of climbers in my day. I'll have you know I was fixing Gestalts long before we first met."

"Ah-ah-ah," Neela said with a click of her tongue. "You said you worked *with* climbers. That means you didn't work *as* a climber."

"Well, it wasn't my *primary* job," Xerx at last admitted with defeat.

"I'm your wife," Neela said. "It's not wise to try to tell me half the truth. Besides, you know there's a reason why climbers are all Felyan."

"Not all of them," he protested while watching the readouts displayed on his pad shift madly. "What about Mobola?"

"She doesn't... oh!" Neela paused for a moment, as a red warning appeared on Xerx's pad: something that certainly was reflected on his wife's end. "Got it. There's a jumper loose on the muscle latency compensator. It must've taken a hit in your last match."

"Don't change the subject," Xerx said, setting to work on the area Neela had indicated. You don't *have* to be Felyan to be a climber."

"No, but even you will agree that their agility really helps. The only reason Mobola gets away with it is she's a genius. She'll run a rep job *solo* ... and she does all the calculations on her handheld, with no bionics." Xerx's pad flashed a blue light, indicating that Neela had set to reprogramming the nanogel. "If you'd have let her stay planetside, we'd be done by now."

"She's better needed on the ship," Xerx said. "And genius doesn't even cover it. Try savant." At that moment, Xerx thought about the painfully shy girl, wondering if she worked solo because it was more efficient or because she was truly that socially awkward. "She needs to learn to live a little, though. Besides, Pepper would have never forgiven me if I left her with ..."

Neela interrupted. "The poor boy! You shouldn't get his hopes up."

"Hey, I don't tell him anything," Xerx protested. "It's up to him and you-know-who if and when that happens."

"You still don't have to play cupid's middleman," Neela warned. "Mobola is afraid of her own shadow right now; she's lost so much."

"What better thing to boost her confidence?" Xerx countered, undaunted. "I'm aware as anyone about how she took the news of Mandela I's annexation." His voice softened. "I had to console you as well, remember?"

"Yes, but that was—"

"*Kidege* ..." Xerx stressed the term of endearment with uncharacteristically sincere gentleness. "I'm serious. This plan might be good for her and Pepper both. Besides, Isibar did it for us."

There was a long pause before Neela replied, her tone reluctant. "That's ... true. But now you owe him a pirate's bounty on some mad scientist's head," Neela countered.

"Considering what she did to him, not to mention to the Felyans, I think it's well deserved," Xerx said. "I'd go through hell and back for that man for bringing us together, you know." He grinned slyly. "Or are you saying that you regret it?"

Neela's giggle rang over the comm and throughout the acoustics of the hangar. "Oh, my cheeky husband! I will have to make you pay for that later."

"I look forward to it." Xerx's voice was heavy with expectation.

Loudly and abruptly, the door buzzer broke into their conversation.

"Shit," Xerx hissed. He placed his tools down on the flattest part of the arm's surface he could find and reached for the controls for the hoist.

"It's alright," Neela said. "I'm closer to the elevator." But Xerx had already committed himself—which was probably why he had failed to realize that he'd pressed the wrong button on the control wand. No sooner than he slid off the edge, he noticed that the hoist was pulling him up instead of down, ultimately suspending him awkwardly head over heels, his leg tangled in a section of the harness, which remained that way for the remainder of his slow descent. Spotting his wife directly below, he scowled at her echoing giggle and amused grin. She idly played with the thick braid that she had woven from the hair that grew at the base of her otherwise bald scalp, and then, with large brown eyes that sparkled with mischief, watched the machine slowly bring him down the final few feet. She pressed the stop button on the controls once he was level with her arms and held him in a manner similar to the way he carried her over the threshold of the *Reckless*' dropship on their wedding day.

"Very funny," Xerx said as Neela unwrapped the section of the harness from his leg. She then restarted the hoist to bring him the rest of the way down. He cast her a lopsided grin in spite of himself as he set both feet on the ground. "You must've wanted to do that for years."

"I plead my right to silence," Neela purred, touching her nose against his own: a prelude to a kiss that perhaps lingered too long, as the buzzer again sounded, three times in a row, and far more insistent.

"Someone's impatient," Xerx commented, eliciting an amused snort from his wife. "Go on ahead; I have the rest."

Neela hurried off toward the main office door at the far end of the hangar while Xerx unbuckled himself, taking care to not become tangled in yet another embarrassing way. It was slow going, but he managed to at last wrest himself free of the rigging of cables and clasps.

"Geez, it wasn't this hard getting into it," he muttered, reaching for his jacket that he'd left hanging by the edge of a nearby tool rack. He paused to glance upward with a smile at his titanic prize-winning machine. *Imani* resembled a knight in full armor, its panels forming geometric patterns that glinted in the hangar's harsh overhead lights. A relic of the Imperium Wars of centuries past, she was truly a work of art: not cobbled together from deep space battle remnants, but rather, a true refurbished original, and thus worth a small fortune.

This had better be important, he thought as he followed Neela's path toward the office.

Well, it certainly seemed important.

Xerx shuddered inwardly when he noticed the condition of their guest occupying a corner of the desk with Neela, but he forced a smile as he quickened his pace toward the man who sat hugging a mug of coffee as if it were a lover.

"Gregor," Xerx said, trying to sound upbeat. Their Gestalt team's tool provider was lanky and pale, with falls of scraggly, half-grayed, dirty brown hair, and was shaking like a leaf. He always looked like he would blow away in a stiff breeze, but he usually carried himself with an air of unflappable confidence. Still, he had never before seemed so shaken. Neela hovered beside him, a look of concern on her face, and most alarmingly, a pistol in her hand. Without a word, she locked eyes with him, then glanced pointedly at the window behind the desk.

As he approached the pair, Xerx inspected Gregor's haunted gaze. He caught the MAG pistol that Neela had tossed him from the open weapons cabinet. With a combination of trained hand and reflex, he chambered the ammo rounds and switched off the safety.

"What's going on here?" he asked.

"He was near to babbling when he came in," Neela said, her voice a low conspiratorial register, "but from what I got from it, he says he's being hunted."

Gregor then cast a gentle, yet clear silencing gesture her way.

"Thank you, Neela," his voice came in a slightly quavering whisper. He swallowed, then exhaled loudly, "but I think I've reached ... words again. I can explain it."

"Explain what?" Xerx asked. He had been about to click the safety back into place and slip the gun into the secret holster in the back part of his pants, but Gregor grabbed his wrist, stopping him.

"I wouldn't put that thing away just yet," Gregor said. "You're going to need it after what I have to say."

TWO

"They're after me," Gregor said.

"Who's after you?" Xerx asked.

"His former employers," Neela was still glancing furtively out the nearby window. "Or at least, he thinks that's it."

"I hope you're not calling me a liar," Gregor said, sounding stricken.

"Never." Xerx frowned, confused at how Gregor could be worried about something that was, as far as he knew, ancient history. "But you haven't heard from MTHI in over a decade." He watched as the scraggly-looking man's gaze drifted back to the black contents of his mug.

"They chased my ass all over the colonies before my ... well, the people who got me out managed to shake them."

"Again, a decade ago," Xerx said, his tone somewhat less patient. But Gregor continued undaunted.

"I thought I was careful, you know. I didn't always look like a reject from a space hippie fleet. But when the mercs stowed me away here, I got me some surgery that even bounty hunters couldn't see through. I thought they'd given up. I thought I wasn't *that* valuable to them."

"And only now, you think someone ratted you out?" Xerx found himself stifling his urge to pistol whip the man.

Gregor shrugged. "Maybe someone's got good eyes. Or maybe a Felyan or hybrid I worked with caught my scent; how should I know?"

Xerx, thankful that Neela could pick up on his growing annoyance, came to the window beside her, trying to put some distance between himself and Gregor. Outside, their massive transport truck was parked under the streetlamps' harsh light. Half a mile away was the tarmac where the dropship to the *Reckless* was parked, alongside the hangars for the other teams and their Gestalts. He saw no suspicious movement, but that didn't exactly mean anything.

"Were they close by?" his wife asked, changing the subject.

"I think I lost them in the storage sheds around my shop," Gregor said. "Whoever they were, they weren't all that skilled."

"Or maybe they intentionally led you here," Xerx remarked.

"And you're sure they're from your old employer?" Neela asked.

"Who else could they be?" Gregor looked almost insulted.

"Gregor, you know that MTHI doesn't do anything half-assed," Neela reminded him. "If they wanted you, we wouldn't be able to stop them."

Gregor took a larger swallow of the coffee, grimacing as if he'd drank something more akin to the more rancid homemade kombuchas from the bazaar. Shaking it off, he looked at Neela with bleary eyes that seemed to at last grasp what she was suggesting. "Wait. You're saying that these guys aren't from my old company?"

"She's probably right," Xerx answered, shoving back his urge to huff out his frustration. Gregor was a good person, but fear did often drive him to forge these chains of irrational logic. However, this sequence of events did awaken a concern of his own. "Look, if they wanted you that badly, you'd already be tranqed and halfway to Dorado."

"Halfway to Dorado in a crate aboard the *Shadow Star*, most likely," Neela interjected.

Xerx nodded. "Yeah, Paige doesn't fuck around with stuff like that." Paige and her crew were MTHI's gophers who always got their pound of flesh.

"Then ... who the hell is after me, if not them?" Gregor said.

"Someone with a lot of data on you in order to make it look legit," Xerx replied.

"Perhaps five someones?" Neela said. "All wearing diffraction cloth?"

"Sh-*Shit!*" Gregor sputtered, standing bolt upright. Practically kicking the chair away from the table, he staggered to the side and backed up toward the wall. Then, with a sound metallic *thud*, slumped to the floor, unconscious.

Neela, who had still been keeping an eye on their encroaching guests, turned away from the window, startled at the noise. "What happened to him?" she asked, seeing Gregor's motionless form.

"Hit his head on the weapons' safe," Xerx gestured to the sturdy locker directly above the spot where their friend had collapsed. "Probably for the best, though. At least one problem solved itself."

"They're just standing there now," Neela said, returning her attention to the outside.

"Got a bad feeling," Xerx said. "This is too convenient."

"Do you believe Gregor now?" Neela asked, confused.

"No, but it's not the only factor here," Xerx replied. "And it's kind of funny you mentioned it a few minutes ago. Last year when Isibar visited, he told me he was closing in on ... well, on *her*."

"Wait, *her*?" Neela said, casting one more furtive glance outside. "But she wouldn't know you're here. And even if she did, she's left you alone for years."

"For years, my cousin was following a cold trail," Xerx said. "And from what he told me, this person has a thing for being proactive."

"Yes, but you have no way of knowing—"

"You're right," Xerx said. "I don't. But it's a bit more plausible than Gregor's cockamamie story."

"Not by much," Neela said, sounding unconvinced. "Well, our guests, whoever sent them, don't look like they're going anywhere. Should we at least entertain them?"

"I can take 'em all, you know," Xerx said, conceding to his wife's skepticism. He decided to put a pin in his theory for now, as he unclasped the strap to the holster on the second pistol he kept at his thigh. Neela fixed him with a worried look.

"*Kipenzi*, I don't think that is a good idea," she said.

"You're cute when you worry." Xerx fixed his wife with a sweet look as he returned to the weapons locker and punched in the combination. He then removed an EM grenade along with a launcher extension. "Besides, I'm out of practice."

"At least let me get to the ship," Neela said. She nodded toward Gregor. "Will he be okay?"

"He'll be fine." Xerx gave a carefree smile. "Now, here's the plan: I'll provide a distraction; you make for the Grasshopper."

Neela scowled. "That isn't very comforting."

"Wasn't meant to be." Xerx discreetly slid open the window, then shoved the grenade into the launcher's barrel. "But I'll be careful." He paused, then addressed the building's A.I.

"CAINA, kill the lights."

The sight of Neela approaching him was the last thing that Xerx saw before the room was shrouded in darkness, followed by a quick, gentle press of her lips upon his own.

"When are you ever careful?" she asked.

"No choice but to believe me, though."

"No, I guess not." He heard her sigh as he peered through the window, took careful aim, then cursed under his breath. He could see the distortions but lacked his wife's more trained eye to tell where one ended and the other began. "Are they all still just standing there?"

There was a pause as he waited for Neela to study the situation. Finally, she answered, "Yes. Seems like they're waiting for us to make the first move."

"Good. Do your stuff, and I'll do mine."

He heard her footsteps as she jogged off, followed by the closing of the office door. Then he proceeded to count. He couldn't number their guests, but the grenade and its short-range EM pulse would fix that very quickly.

"... eight, nine, ten."

He pulled the trigger.

In hindsight, Xerx wished he hadn't peeked out the window just before the EM blast hit. It worked as planned; the diffraction cloth's light distortion fell away like fragments of a hologram, leaving the company visible, the entire assembly looking like ninjas in burqas. However, the electrical flash had been bright enough to momentarily blur his vision. He'd staggered out to the door and let fly with his gun, but only nailed two by his reckoning before he could dive behind a nearby power box. A sparse hail of MAG rounds flew over his head, and he tossed a magnesium flare he'd pilfered from the office their way. As he hoped, the company scattered, thinking it was an explosive, and Xerx fled in the opposite direction, regretting not having counted their numbers. A block down the road and counting proved to be a moot point, as distortions of more camouflaged assailants dove off of the rooftops.

Xerx blindly fired multiple MAG rounds at the distortions, taking advantage of their sudden arrival to catch them off guard. It seemed to work for only one; he believed he saw him crumble to the ground, but the cloth's light-bending qualities made it impossible to be sure. He found himself again diving for cover from another volley of MAG rounds—some of which just missed him as he took a chance and sprinted away, making an abrupt 90-degree turn into a nearby narrow alley.

It was a service alley between stores: long, with multiple piled crates for cover, and its width making a good bottleneck to take out any pursuers ... but after making considerable distance, his heartbeat slowed, and he became more aware of the lack of sound. Diffraction cloth didn't muffle sound, and there was little else but the sound of spider crickets singing to break the dead silence. In the dead center of the alley, Xerx's fear gave way to confusion, and then he took a more strategic stock of his surroundings.

The opposite end of the alley seemed to lead to an open court: the perfect place for an ambush if his pursuers chose to take an alternate route to cut him off. *Probably not a good idea then*, Xerx thought. He glanced back the way he came. *But where to go now?*

A horrible thought nearly stopped his heart.

"Neela!" he whispered in a choked voice.

Had they abandoned their pursuit for her instead? He would never forgive himself if that was the case. His mind racing, he quickly made a plan. With questionable routes both ahead and behind, there was nowhere else to go but up. He then leaped atop a nearby air conditioning unit that reached the eaves of the building and pulled himself to the low rooftop. Gaining his footing, Xerx waited, listening for any sounds of pursuit. But even atop the corrugated steel and stone rooftops that composed Pit Town, the warm night was clear and just as silent.

"This is crazy," he at last murmured aloud. "Where the hell did they all go?"

Holstering his pistols, he oriented himself toward his team's hangar in the GI yards, which towered over the rooftops. The "Supremacy of God" *Adinkra* symbol that composed Team *Imani*'s logo was spray-painted prominently upon its massive rolling door. On a flat-out run, it would be five minutes to the tarmac from the hangar, even leaping from rooftop to rooftop.

Fear for his wife overrode the questionable logic of his plan, and he set off back the way he came, speeding toward the location of the Grasshopper, praying under his breath that Neela had managed to get the vessel airborne before anyone could reach her.

Funny how everyone has a plan until they get punched in the face.

The old saying reverberated in Xerx's head after the smart blow to his side, which sent him flying to the ground and skidding halfway across the rooftop.

A harsh force from invisible hands attempted to restrain him as he ground to a halt, but he forced them away, giving himself enough time to draw his knife. As the diffraction cloth depowered, he pressed the blade against the neck of his assailant: female, he guessed by the slight stature—it was too dark to make out any secondary sexual characteristics—but he could definitely feel the blade that she pressed against his neck in turn.

Something on the assailant's body glinted in the faint light of the three moons, partly hidden by the cloak but not well enough. Silver as the ambient light, the insignia's appearance was unmistakable: a curving "C" shape, with an end like an open-mouthed serpent, about to swallow a large circle, and a smaller one on the outside of its tail end.

"Imperials!" Xerx wheezed.

THREE

"Okay, let's not be too hasty here," Xerx started to ease back with his blade, but the assailant kept the pressure with hers. "Look," he said, finally settling on what to say, even though he didn't believe the story personally, "just what do you want with Old Gregor anyway?"

At last, he felt the blade's pressure lessen. For several tense moments, they remained frozen that way, eyes locked upon one another, negotiating wordlessly, Xerx's hearing attuning to his heartbeat in the silence of the sleeping Pit Town.

Suddenly, and most unexpectedly, the assailant began to laugh. At least the female timbre of her voice confirmed her gender.

"Um, did I say something funny?" Xerx's adrenaline high gave way to an awkward feeling of self-consciousness.

"Gregor Paulette?" The assailant repeated the name as a question so distinct, it was as if she was tasting the name for the depths of its potential for scorn. "That lanky has-been? Whatever makes you think we're after him?"

"So you want me?" Xerx said, a curious grin stretching out on the edge of his mouth in spite of his disquiet. Had his prior supposition been right? "Whatever happened to just spiking a guy's drink?"

With a smile that Xerx could only barely make out, the girl shook the concealing hood off her head. He wasn't sure why, but he expected to see the pale skin and monochromatic hair of an

Imperial tank, though the Second Imperium wasn't known for using what amounted to shock troops for small-time kidnapping jobs, especially this far outside their territory. Rather, he was greeted by an unexpectedly young-looking face with skin tones that were quite human, crowned with long blue hair tied into complicated braids that seemed to emit an eerie glow. Her large golden eyes held an almost feral intensity. But most prominent of all was the eerily familiar shape of her face and placement of its features.

Xerx pondered this turn of events during the significant pause between himself and the girl. Whoever she was, or wherever she'd come from, Xerx knew a fake-out when he saw it. Though she wore an Imperial insignia, this girl wasn't part of an Imperial team … not an official one, at least.

The sound of approaching footsteps ended his silent reverie, along with the quick back fist he struck into the girl's abdomen. The second Xerx heard his would-be attacker crumple to the ground, he leaped back as if on spring-loaded bionics, putting a quick distance between the girl and himself.

It wasn't enough, he quickly discovered, as the girl recovered from his blow with inhuman speed, then rushed forward, slicing at him, her blade catching his own wildly flung parry, which caused Xerx's grip on the knife's handle to falter. As he struck the ground, he heard it clatter away, impossibly out of reach. On instinct, his opposite hand moved to the holster at his hip but was quickly restrained by a second knife that had appeared from out of nowhere. He felt the sting of its edge barely graze his arm as it tore through the blue leather of his jacket sleeve, wedging itself into the rooftop. His other arm was pinned down with a great deal more pain as her shin struck the ground and wedged it to his side, pressing into the bicep. Xerx snarled as he felt the bruising impact. She might not have been a tank, but it all happened with near-blinding speed. There was no way that this girl could not have been wired with some serious hardware.

THREE

"You know ... in my younger days..." Xerx began, now noticing the skin-tight build of the girl's half-concealed uniform beneath the cloak, but her blade, again placed unceremoniously against his neck, silenced him.

"You talk too much," the woman hissed, hovering directly above.

"I've been told that," Xerx said as the footsteps came closer and then stopped: a mysterious company having gathered around him. A peculiar, yet familiar chemical odor accosted his nostrils: *phaed*, no doubt: a neurotoxin he'd remembered from an apothecary on An'Re'Hara. It was used amongst mercs and pirates, coated on knife blades when a mission required the target to be taken alive. Consecutively, at the edge of his vision, he caught a hand that held a set of very uncomfortable-looking handcuffs.

But as he had been about to consign himself to his fate, yet another sound came to his awareness: a sound that flooded him with a radiant sense of combined relief and impending victory.

A laugh wobbled up unbidden from his stomach with the sound's rapid approach. As if they had been relieved of temporary deafness, it took about two seconds after for the entire company to become aware of it. Even the girl had turned her head too late, yet she somehow managed to roll off of him as the dropship swept in low. Xerx squeezed his eyes shut as the Grasshopper's floodlights overpowered the night's faint moonlight, followed by a cacophony of MAG turret fire and hail of hot stone that pelted his face. Distressed shouts quickly transformed into screams, followed by a pall of morbid silence.

"You can get up now, *Kidege*," Neela said, her voice, amplified from the ship's hull. Xerx opened his eyes, making sure everything was intact, then squinted at the floodlights that were still trained on him. The dropship floated before him, buoyed by its antigravs, turret blisters still steaming, and its open ramp hanging down from its side hatch. Three or four bodies lay surrounding him amidst the billowing clouds of dust, all cowled with diffraction cloth cloaks, now torn and bloodied.

"Hurry aboard," Neela's voice took on a higher, more nervous pitch. "A few of them managed to slip away, and they're not showing up locally on the scanner."

Groaning with the pain that still coursed through his arm, Xerx crawled to his feet, teetering with momentary unsteadiness before stalking quickly over to the dropship's waiting ramp. He hefted himself inside, then climbed into the cockpit before stealing a brief, relieved kiss from his wife.

"Not a second too soon," he said, wanting nothing more than to find some secluded corner to hold her possessively for the rest of the night. But for now, he just wanted to return to where he was needed.

"Looks like they weren't after Gregor," Neela observed.

"No shit." Xerx bleated out a humorless chuckle while adjusting the co-pilot's chair, his voice grim. "Somebody wants a piece of my ass, and not in the best-girl-in-the-brothel kind of way."

"Definitely not good." Neela's expression had faltered into something that was almost blank.

Xerx snorted. "Tell me something I don't know."

"I'm pregnant."

"Not funny," he remarked flatly, in spite of her attempt to lighten the mood. Still, he flashed her a grin for consolation as he double-checked the scanner readouts for any survivors.

"Nothing's out there except a few cold bodies," Neela said. "Somebody's going to have a bad day tomorrow when the heat starts making them smell."

"Better them than me," Xerx remarked. "I don't see any out there that looks like that girl. I don't think she was human."

"What girl?" Neela said.

"The one who had me almost by my balls," Xerx replied. "I think she hauled ass just as you showed up. She had a toxin-coated blade trained on me. She was a lot faster and stronger than she should've been." Xerx frowned, recalling the familiarity of her features. "But her face ..."

"Someone you saw before?" Neela asked.

"Maybe." Xerx shook his head. "She looked so damn familiar. Like ... the right features, but the wrong colors—I don't know." He exhaled loudly, appearing to deflate in his seat. "Probably just my imagination anyway. Screw it. We need to go. If you didn't get 'em all, then I don't think the ones we left alive are too happy. And I'd bet your dowry they have a ship of their own."

"Then we should get back to the *Reckless*?"

"Great minds think alike," Xerx said affectionately as his wife punched instructions into the navigational computer.

"And what about Gregor?" Neela asked.

"I'm pretty sure he'll be okay until the morning," Xerx said. "But he's gonna be pissed we left him behind."

Neela shrugged. "We'll just have to make it up to him later," she said as the vessel began its ascent. Xerx buckled himself in and relaxed, rubbing his face as he shook off the stress of the last several minutes.

"Once I'm on board, I'm gonna have to make a few calls to Iriid," Xerx said, breaking a slight silence that began to hang between them.

"You look unnerved," Neela said, frowning.

"Pissed is more like it," Xerx replied. He might not have been able to figure out who had sent those goons, but now that he had time to breathe, he couldn't help but feel a smoldering rage about the whole affair. Plus, he still had a nagging sense of familiarity from the girl who'd nearly given him a scar to add to his collection. "I've been in the game since before I met you, but my family knows how to play it better than anyone. Both my cousins have a thing about hits on family, and pirates have a long reach. Someone's head is gonna roll, and I'm gonna see to it that it gets displayed from the palace walls on Rhoma."

The chirping of an alarm broke into their conversation. Neela glanced at the radar and stiffened.

"Well, that was quick," she muttered.

"A ship is tailing us, isn't it?" Xerx asked, his voice grim.

"Like stink on a pig," Neela replied as a second alarm chirped at a different pitch. "Too bad we don't have that long reach you spoke of right now."

"Why?"

"Their weapons are armed."

FOUR

"**A**re they freaking *crazy?*" Xerx shrieked at the targeting system holos. The pursuing craft was not at all what he'd expected: a Corax transport, its sleek shape unmistakable, its forward turrets open—

Wait. Turrets? Coraxes didn't have turrets.

"Shit, it's modded! Xerx said through clenched teeth. "Someone strapped MAGs to it." He muted the weapons alarm, silencing its incessant chirp. "I know it's nighttime, but there's still air traffic!"

"I really don't think they care about that," Neela remarked. She hovered her arm above her section of the control console as thin, silvery filaments slipped from the *msaidizi*: a small, green translucent organic-looking device, fused to the flesh on the back of her hand. It spun out the filaments from its gelatinous green dorsal orb, which threaded themselves into a series of sockets at the console's edge. Upon contact, Neela's gaze became unfocused and distant, and a plethora of holos erupted about her.

"Buckle up, honey," she said, her voice now coming in through the ship's audio systems. "I'll risk a ticket and punch the atmospheric boundary here. It'll get us closer to the *Reckless* without needing to double back on legal lanes."

"It might also give them more time to fire at us," Xerx warned.

"Not if we hit them first."

Xerx frowned with dismay at the readouts his console was feeding him, first noting the significant size difference between this ship and the pursuing craft and then its armor component.

"Hate to piss in your corn flakes, *kipenzi*, but I don't think we'll make a respectable dent in them if we emptied all our ammo. It's like a shark chasing a guppy."

"That is why you have the *Reckless*," Neela replied.

"We haven't tested her defense systems yet."

"Never a better time, don't you think?" One of her surrounding holograms slid towards him. The comm icon flashed above the words, CONNECTED TO RECKLESS.

"Grasshopper to *Reckless*," Xerx began, then yelped as he felt Neela give the ship a burst of acceleration. "We're coming in with a bandit on our tail. Salt, track our position for target verification. Weapons free."

The face of a middle-aged An'Kya Felyan appeared, nearly filling the screen. His dirty gray-white hair surrounded a chiseled face, banded by stripes that were a darker shade than his hair.

"Salt, you're too close to the damn screen," Xerx said.

"Atmospheric boundary reached," Neela said just before another alarm sounded. "They're firing."

"Bad news, captain," Salt said, backing away from the screen.

Xerx threw up his hands, making a disgusted noise. "Lemme guess. Weapons aren't working?"

"My idiot son had to take them offline for his work," Salt replied as Xerx gripped the weapons controls. He traced the targeting reticle to the image of the ship in the hologram below and squeezed the trigger. As a part of him expected, much to his chagrin, the computer registered negative contacts.

"Then tell Pepper to bring them back online," Xerx said, feeling a headache begin to develop in his temples. He fired another impotent volley before giving up. "How long will that take?"

"Depends on how long he can keep his nose out of that spazzy human girl's—"

"Salt! Focus!"

"Evasive maneuvers," Neela announced. "Hang on." Xerx immediately felt the massive G-forces shove his right shoulder and arm uncomfortably into the harness. He gritted his teeth through the pain and fired yet another impotent volley at the pursuing vessel. "Look, we're coming in hot; can you at least have the hangar bay doors open?"

"On it," he said. He began barking orders in Felyan off-screen before the video feed cut.

"And for the love of God, try to get those damn guns online!"

"Concussive rounds," his wife said at the tail end of yet another shrill alarm, and the ship rocked with vibrations that Xerx could feel in his teeth. It then dawned on him that these shots weren't being aimed directly their way. A Corax might be slower on acceleration, but they could easily outpace them given enough time, and he had a suspicion that its weapons loadout was higher caliber than their own. And that little adventure in Pit Town had been evidence enough that taking them out clearly wasn't the plan. The hits had been precise and just close enough for concussive force to rattle them. Circuitry could only take so much abuse before something broke and left them dead in the water. He watched and braced himself again as the ship rattled, and a light show of explosions burst in an almost floral pattern about the ship.

"They're trying to swat us out of the sky," Xerx concluded.

"If one is a TIP, then we're screwed," Neela remarked, as if they needed more bad news. "Worst. Date. Ever."

Xerx couldn't help but chuckle at the ill-timed joke before another jarring rattle cut him short. He released the ship's limited supply of countermeasures to buy them some time.

"What's our ETA?" he said.

"Thirty seconds," Neela said, "and we're coming in way too fast. Orbital guard must be sitting on their collective thumbs to ignore this kind of light show."

Another, more powerful jarring rattle caused Xerx to feel as if he'd been thrown into a can of dry beans. Alarm klaxons blared, and the words, DIRECT HIT. HULL DAMAGE, appeared in flashing red holograms.

"Shit!"

Xerx gave a mild start at the expletive. Rarely did Neela curse unless it was something *really* bad. "Damage right above our port wing, near the fuel tank," he heard her say.

"Damn! That was right on the knuckle," Xerx observed.

"Any deeper, and we'd be scattered into orbiting debris," was his wife's morose reply. A green holo appeared in front of her otherwise blank expression, showing the glyph for the fire suppression system. "Rerouting power; systems stabilizing ... for now."

"Salt, where are those guns?" Xerx nearly shouted his demand into the comm. "These guys mean business!"

"We're trying, Captain. Almost got it!" came Salt's gruff voice. He chattered in Felyan to his crewmate, Var'Rakeska, who had remained off-screen. The Hara'Kya Felyan answered back in like language.

"Then do a full reboot, Var!" he yelled over Salt's attempt to respond. "It'll make no difference if it works or not if we're dead!"

The dropship shook once again, but this time not as severely, as the computer registered another concussive round ... then another, and another. Xerx returned fire—perhaps only to make himself feel better.

"I have the *Reckless* in sight," Neela said. Xerx looked upward, through the forward viewport. The vessel sat high above: a rectangular profile with forward-facing wings, flecked with lights, small at first, but growing larger at a painfully slow rate as Neela angled the dropship's approach vector toward the hangar. It was hard to believe they were pushing nearly five klicks a second. Another hit sent his insides shaking, and another flurry of holos blocked his view.

"Lemme guess," Xerx said amidst the alarms, "starboard side this time?"

"They want us in one piece after all." It was as if Neela had only just now come to his own prior conclusion.

"One very battered piece but intact nonetheless," Xerx said, his face fixed in a frown. "At least I know I'm that valuable to them." He thought it was odd that the bandit hadn't used a TIP. The EM blast from any Tactical Ion Pulse missiles would short out the dropship's systems. Maybe they didn't have one after all? "I think I have a plan, though."

"What kind of plan?" Neela asked, her voice now coming through the ship's audio. Her gaze remained eerily trained upon the nothingness that was the data feed in her mind, but there was a definite note of skepticism in her tone in addition to her expression of disquiet.

"When the approach vector is fully angled, decelerate," Xerx said. If you're right, and they use a TIP, we can still make it, with the *Reckless'* help or not."

"I don't like that plan, *kipenzi*," Neela's large brown eyes momentarily focused on him, full of genuine worry. "I *really* don't like that plan."

"I don't either," Xerx said, as his face betrayed a humorless smile. "But if you've got a better one—"

"No, no." Neela's gaze once again fell into a contemplation of the data that fed into her mind. "I was just letting you know." A moment later, she heaved a deep sigh, both bodily, and through the system. "Decelerating. Vector complete."

Xerx fired off several more impotent volleys at the pursuing Corax. "Now, act like we're doing evasive maneuvers. Hopefully, they won't get too suspicious of our deceleration. With any luck, they should—"

The ship shuddered once again, and Neela gave a painful yelp. Xerx saw the threads from the *msaidizi* on her hand buckle and retract with flashing discharges arcing from the sockets. The holos unceremoniously vanished, and every readout on every screen flickered off. He reached over to his wife, giving a wordless look of concern.

"I'm all right," she whispered, massaging the hand upon which the plant-like device rested. "It was just a little shock."

"Guess they had a TIP after all," Xerx said quietly, looking about the now darkened cockpit. "Trajectory's good; now here's hoping we can coast the rest of the way in."

Several blinding flashes erupted from the *Reckless*, and Xerx felt a distant rumble.

"It looks like your system reboot worked," Neela said with an air of satisfaction. At least the bandit was no longer a concern.

"About damn time," Xerx muttered.

Several seconds passed and Xerx sat with his wife, cautiously optimistic, yet smiling at a job well done. But their peaceful moment was cut jarringly short, as Xerx felt another rattling vibration, accompanied soon after by a feeling of strong forces shoving them nearly sideways in their seats, their restraining harnesses again digging into their flesh.

"Something must have hit us," Neela said.

"Something big," Xerx added. He strained, reaching for the comm switch, at first forgetting that the EM pulse had taken it out. He then switched on his personal comm, hoping he was now within range. A moment later, Salt's voice came through, though flecked with static.

"Is that you, Captain?"

Xerx opened his mouth to make a sarcastic remark but thought better of it. "Yeah, thanks for the save. They hit us with a TIP. We're dead in space, but we've got the trajectory to the hangar bay down pat. Debris from the bandit hit us in the rear, though, and it has us spinning. Ready the crash systems for impact."

"Crash systems ready," Salt replied, this time with more confidence than their prior conversation.

Out the sides of the viewport, Xerx watched as debris from the destroyed Corax scattered in various directions, moving away from them, some in actual flames that quickly sputtered out in the vacuum, and others merely glowing a dull red with their dying heat as they drifted off into the void. The *Reckless* was still spinning, now a massive vessel above, with flashing running lights leading into the open maw of the hangar bay before them, the dropship still the captive of centrifugal forces as it careened toward its destination.

"Have the crash systems been checked?" Neela asked in the silence.

Xerx bit his lip, feeling a pit collapse in his stomach.

"No."

Seconds passed like minutes. Then suddenly, they were enveloped by the rim of the hangar bay. Xerx glanced at the velocity gauge and gasped.

"Brace yourself!" Xerx warned. He crossed his arms over his chest and took hold of two straps of the harness. Afterward, he did the only thing he could do and rarely ever did: pray.

It was as if he were a rock thrown into an unbalanced washing machine, the forces tearing at him from all sides were shaking, jerking, jostling, and juddering, combined with horrifying screeching noises as the wounded vessel no doubt tumbled across the runway. For one horrible second, Xerx guessed with dismay that the crash systems hadn't worked after all. So, in a moment of numb fatalism, he gave himself over to whatever awaited on the other side.

To his absolute astonishment, the violent shaking and shuddering that threatened to shatter every bone in his body only moments before abruptly died away: a cacophony that softened to a deafening silence.

Tentatively, he opened his eyes. At last, confident that he was not dead, he unfurled himself from his protective position and gazed at the viewport, through which he could see nothing, except a sea of white.

"The hell...?"

He felt the pull of the *Reckless'* artificial gravity as he undid the harness and stepped out of his seat with trembling legs. Confident that nothing was broken, he turned around to check on his wife.

His eyes settled on Neela's alarmingly empty seat beside him.

"K-*Kidege*?" he stammered, still ungainly, and feeling himself seize with sudden combined worry and near-terror.

"Heading out," he heard her say from behind him: a sound that gave him a swell of almost dizzying relief. She sounded blessedly unhurt ... and in surprisingly good spirits considering what they'd gone through. Xerx craned his neck toward the back of the cabin and saw his wife heading to the entrance hatch, looking healthy as she sounded. "I'm going to get us out of here."

"Xerx gathered his footing as he followed, ducking beneath exposed wiring and loose overhead panels while nursing a newly discovered bruise beside his knee.

"Are you okay, love?" he heard Neela ask.

"I will be." Xerx nodded, realizing the room had only now just started to spin more slowly. "Let's get the hell outta here."

Neela grabbed the manual controls for the exit hatch and pushed, straining for a moment before there was a cracking noise, coupled with a shower of a powdery white substance before it seemed to jam.

"Well, if you wanted to know if the crash systems still work," Neela said through gritted teeth, "they do!"

Xerx came to her aid and joined his efforts with hers, forcing the hatch the rest of the way open through the hardened foam.

Xerx then pushed against the mass that seemed to block their way, finding it surprisingly pliable and fragile, crumbling after only a firm press. He worked with his wife to dig their way through to the open hangar, then looked back toward the closing doors to see a mess of torn steel and masses of foam floating at the edge of the ship's artificial gravity field. Closer to where they'd landed, the foam lay in sheets of increasing thickness, covering the dropship like poorly applied cake icing. The parts of the vessel's hull that the foam hadn't concealed looked beaten up pretty badly but otherwise seemed potentially salvageable. At least nothing appeared to be on fire.

"Well, that could've gone better," Neela said, slipping her hand into his. She observed the damage, shaking her head ruefully. "This is going be hell to clean up."

Reluctantly, Xerx unfolded their hands, frowning as a disconcerting notion came to mind. "That's the least of my worries, right now," he said, beginning a brisk, purposeful stride toward the elevator. "Come on, we need to get to the bridge." He activated his comm. "We're aboard, Salt, and in one piece, but I've got a feeling we're not out of the fire yet."

He saw Neela open her mouth to protest, then shut it. Even Salt had been conspicuously silent.

"What do you mean?" Salt finally asked over the comm.

"I could be wrong," Xerx admitted, both to his wife and crewmate, "but I don't think we should hang around here to find out."

FIVE

"**H**oney, I think you're being just a little bit paranoid," Neela suggested as the door to the elevator opened. "There was only one ship after us."

"Maybe I am," Xerx said, pursing his lips as he set the bridge as their destination, "but I have a sneaking suspicion that we haven't seen the last of those guys."

"I think you're still worried that it's *her*," Neela said.

Xerx turned to look into his wife's large, dark amber eyes. "Considering how often trouble finds us, can you blame me?" The side of his mouth twitched as he snorted out a tiny laugh. "But I'm not *that* paranoid."

"Not yet, anyway," Neela said, sounding far from comforted. But her tone was at least accepting.

Salt's voice crackled over his comm.

"Captain, we're getting a lot of buzz on the orbital guard bands. Looks like that light show got their attention."

There was a long pause between the two. Xerx surmised that Neela had to keep herself from giggling at the look that was plastered on his face.

"Say it," she said, shaking her head with a rueful grin.

"I hate it when I'm right," Xerx remarked obligingly. "I swear, if any kind of God *is* looking out for me, then his name is Murphy."

He then spoke into the comm. "We're heading up to the bridge, Salt. Fire up the hyperdrive and set a course for ... anywhere but here."

"On it," Salt replied. "Cycling up the drive."

After nearly a minute, the elevator door opened up to the corridor. They passed through the DNA scans of an intermittent series of three force fields, their iridescent sheens switching to the green hue that permitted them to pass through with a cheerful-sounding chime. After the final force field, a blast door opened at the end of the hall, revealing the deceptively expansive environment of the bridge.

Perhaps it was because of the relatively new experience of owning his own ship—a warship of the First Imperium nonetheless—or maybe it was the way the holographic display of the expanse of stars and space traffic above the dominating sphere of Siberna, but the bridge environs had a way of fooling the eye into thinking that it was located somewhere high above the ship. This always seemed to trigger a mild bout of vertigo, which made it difficult for Xerx to walk straight on the incline that led to the command dais or even stand upright without its guide rails. Thankfully, there was a captain's chair for when the dizziness became too much.

"We're moving out of parking orbit now, sir," Salt said as Neela joined him on the platform below. The tactical and helm officer's tail flicked excitedly as he punched in a stream of commands into his console. Xerx watched the surrounding display holo as a series of lines and arrows appeared, indicating the ship's vector away from their position.

"Steady as she goes," he said, adding, "unlike my stomach," under his breath as a wave of dizziness caught him. He reminded himself to ask Var to blend him something for vertigo later as the ship began following the indicated course.

"Orbital guard hasn't spotted us, have they?" he asked as the glowing tan, green, and blue orb of Siberna moved away, making way for the field of stars beyond.

"Doubtful that they will, Captain." The reply came from Var. His furry, elongated orange head popped up from the console; he'd been hunched over on the starboard side. "Ships of the First Imperium are built with stuff that trumps current Alliance and Second Imperium tech by several decades."

"She keeps a low sensor profile, and the hull is RAM coated," Neela reminded him. "The only way they'll be able to target us is line-of-sight."

"That's a relief," Xerx replied, reminding himself to catch up with the ship's schematics. It would, after all, be embarrassing to have his crew know more about his ship than he did. "I still think we should get the hell out of here, though." He shifted his gaze back toward Salt. "How long 'til the engines fire up?"

"We have some weird readings coming in from engineering, but—"

"How. Long?"

"Ah, ten seconds," Salt replied stiffly.

"Good," Xerx said, grasping hold of the rails of the dais. "The sooner we get out of here, the better. I'll—"

"Wait!"

Everyone turned to face the open elevator door, where Pepper and Mobola fell through, hand in hand, the charcoal gray-haired Felyan bracing himself against a bulkhead. Mobola stumbled forward, but Pepper caught her, grabbing her across her waist with his tail.

"Shut it off!" he wailed. "Shut it all off!"

"Too late," Var replied, frowning, glancing over at Salt's screen. "Hyperdrive is engaged ..."

Several klaxons blared at once as the field of stars exploded into shifting hues of blue and white: the corridors of hyperspace. Xerx nearly stumbled over the railing as the ship gave a great forward lurch. He heard Mobola and Pepper cry out followed by several hard bumping noises before things settled, and he felt it was safe to move again.

"Var. Salt. Turn that noise off," he said, running down the ramp and to the control console area below. Once he'd hit the floor level, the klaxons silenced, but he knew that things were nowhere near well. They'd made it into hyperspace, but the ambient hum of the hyperdrive that he could usually hear through the deck plates was mysteriously absent.

Neela was pulling Mobola to her feet as Xerx approached them. The younger girl, with darker skin than his wife, was petite in stature, and always looked like a deer in headlights, but though unhurt, she seemed even more the worse for wear than usual.

"What the hell happened?" Xerx asked. "Are you two okay?"

Mobola nodded, but before anyone could speak, Pepper launched himself to his feet and reared up. He looked furious enough to spit fire as his glare locked directly onto Salt.

"Trisii's love, dad! You could have killed us!" The look in his eyes could have torn clean through the ship's outer hull. "Mobola and I were working on the hyperdrive field generator when it powered up. Or did you forget?"

"Wait," Xerx interjected. Nonplussed, he could only stare blankly at the older Felyan. "You forgot your son was working on the hyperdrive?"

Salt stammered at first before he managed to utter anything coherent. When he did, it came out in a mawkish, high-pitched tone. "Look, Captain, when we started tracking you, it was crazy up here." He wrung his hands as he shifted his eyes from Xerx back to his son. "I didn't know you were taking the thing apart, Yari; I thought you said you were only doing a diagnostic."

"An *internal* diagnostic!" Pepper barked. "You usually take things apart for that. "It's only because Mobola had been inter-faced with the locks that we were able to prevent the whole engineering deck from exploding!"

"So why didn't you use the comm?" Salt snapped back. "You could've called a stop to it!"

"I *did!*" Pepper was utterly livid, his tail bushy and straight, his mane of charcoal hair looking wilder than normal. "I practically screamed at you to shut it down! Did you mute the internal comms again?"

Xerx assumed by Salt's imperious look, that he had been about to warn his son to not use that tone of voice. But then, it became quickly apparent, seeing how it deflated under the younger Felyan's admonishment, that his near-fatal gaffe had been inexcusable.

"You muted the comm?" Xerx said flatly.

"Only after your last message," Salt replied. "Once I knew you were safely on the ship, I had a feeling you were going to want us to get out of here, so I was warming up the main engines. I didn't want any distractions; I was going to switch it back on as soon as I was done."

"Good God..." Neela whispered.

"I told you that wasn't a good idea," Var interjected, earning him a withering look from Salt. Var, more resembling a striped wolf, would certainly have looked more menacing if he had been the one giving such a gaze, but the more human-like An'Kya Felyan was not to be underestimated.

"Okay, time out!" Xerx said, forcing his way into the midst of the burgeoning kerfuffle. First of all, Salt, don't get pissed at Var. It's your own fault this happened—" he indicated the projections of the kaleidoscopic swirls of hyperspace in the surrounding holos, "—whatever this is. Seriously, on what planet did you think that turning off the comms was a good thing?" He then turned to the younger Felyan, who still looked angry enough to spit magma. "Pepper, calm down. So you're saying you didn't get the chance to fix it completely?"

"Of course not! We had to get out before patching everything up," Pepper replied, still simmering. "We were only able to plug the most necessary things back in."

"Define 'plugging,'" Xerx said.

"We reconnected the power distribution nodes," Pepper replied.

"But nothing was calibrated," Mobola added, speaking for the first time.

"Well, is it safe to go back?" Neela asked.

"It should be," Mobola's voice was low, quiet, and retained a slight tremble. "I managed to lock the more dangerous conduits down, but if we don't fix the rest soon..."

Xerx nodded, then exhaled, as if he'd been holding it in for hours. "At least you two are safe. First things first, it looks like the main problem might have solved itself. Any of you hear the hyper-drive running?"

Everyone stood quietly for several seconds. Pepper frowned, then turned toward Mobola, who, after glancing around with a puzzled look, shook her head. Even Salt and Var seemed confused, shifting their gazes back and forth toward the nearest bulkhead and then to the surrounding holograms.

It was Neela who voiced her observation.

"I don't think any problem was solved, *kipenzi*. If we're still in hyperspace and the engines are off, that's not good."

"Not good at all," Pepper added redundantly.

"Then we know what we need to tackle first," Xerx remarked. "I'm pretty sure those alarms that went off weren't to say we won the Pit Town lotto." He nodded toward Var, who seemed oddly a statue. "Var, quit spacing out," he said, switching to Felyan. "What have we got?"

"Shouldn't you ask the helmsman?" Var, somewhat confused, gestured toward Salt. "Kyori is better at this."

"I'd rather hear your thoughts on it," Xerx answered. He refrained from admitting his shaken faith in the older Felyan due to his massive faux pas, but the way the Salt avoided eye contact was telling enough. "Pepper, help him out, will you?"

Var shrugged as Pepper came to his side. They conversed in like language as the Hara'Kya Felyan ran his clawed fingers over the controls at his console, his brow furrowed as deeply as that of his An'Kya Felyan cousin. Eventually, his frown deepened to where it looked less like concentration and more like a snarl.

"Bad news, Captain," Pepper said, switching back to Alliance Common. Var sat on his haunches, a scowl affixed to his muzzle. "The Hyperdrive appears to be locked out."

"No surprise there," Xerx said as he eyed the hologram of the outside environs. He noticed a warning icon flashing on the forward-facing image. Beneath it the words, FAILSAFE PROTOCOL INITIATED, flashed. "The question is: how do we unlock them? And by the way," he gestured toward the flashing words on the holo, "anyone know what this is?

"I might've seen something like that while reading the schematics," Mobola chimed in. "Give me a moment." She seated herself before a nearby console and extended her hand. A series of silvery filaments, similar to the threads that spun from Neela's *msaidizi* unfurled from a hole atop her gloved hands, which shunted themselves into the console's interface ports. The screen, in turn, came alive with blueprints and readouts, flashing faster than anyone could read. Mobola stood perfectly still, her eyes rolled back as the computer cycled through an incomprehensible amount of data. At last, she gasped, blinking rapidly, the screen stopping on a readout with words that Xerx was too far away to see.

"I found it," Mobola said ... and then blanched. "The ship's automated systems prevented an explosion in engineering."

"Wish we'd have known that," Pepper sounded nowhere near as disturbed by this news as he probably should have. "Now I feel kinda stupid for getting us out of there so fast."

"The hyperdrive's activation kicked off a power surge," Mobola continued. "The energy was re-routed into the ship by activating something called 'garrison mode.'"

"Even I haven't heard of that one," Neela replied. She swept her gaze across the crew and was met by shrugs or blank looks from all but Mobola.

"All I got about it is that it was used to temporarily house army divisions for swift transport," Mobola explained. "How a power surge activated it, I couldn't find out."

"Is there anything you *did* find out?" Xerx asked.

"We ... need to go to engineering to fix it," Mobola replied, her voice shaking slightly at his impatient tone. "We have to do a cold restart."

"If that's the case, then we'd better do it quickly," Var announced. "Yari and I managed to plot our position, and the hyperspace weather just showed anomalous readings. We're drifting right now and headed toward the Deadlands Expanse. That's right in the gravitational shadow of the Rickman's Pulsar. I don't think any of us want to be crushed into the size of an atom today."

Another klaxon broke in before Xerx could give a single order. And this time, his anger boiled over.

"Dammit, what *now?*" he snapped, throwing his hands in the air.

The ship appeared to answer for him, as he cast his gaze back toward the hologram display. From the surrounding holograms and consoles, in bright red letters, the words, INTRUDER ALERT, flashed from every angle.

"Oh, this day just fucking sucks," he groaned.

SIX

Time was now of the essence, making the ten-minute wait for Mobola to ferret out all the data on this "garrison mode" thing seem an eternity. Most would have said that Xerx had average patience, but this exceeded even his limit. He prepared to set off, but Mobola, still connected to the computer's systems, shut the exit door as soon as he opened them.

"Mobola, open the damn door!" Xerx barked, both furious and impotent in that fury as Mobola was still seated at the console, comatose for the moment, the threads from her hand still interlocked with the systems.

"That would not be very wise, Captain," Mobola replied, her voice booming over the comm systems.

"And why is that?" Xerx snapped.

"Told you she was a spazz," he overheard Salt mutter to his son, who hissed in response.

"Because you'll most likely get lost." Mobola's voice sounded about an octave higher, but not shaky as it tended to get when she was startled. Whether this newfound assertiveness was an effect of her interface or not, he couldn't tell. "Garrison mode is more complex than you know."

"I'm not going to get lost in my own—" Xerx suddenly paused mid-sentence. "Wait. What did you find out?"

"Go to the weapons locker," Mobola answered. "I've requisitioned the proper tools for you."

"She's disconnecting," Neela announced as the filaments retracted into Mobola's hand. Xerx watched as the younger girl stirred awake in the chair, then leaned forward to clutch her head.

"I'm okay," she said, waving Neela off from her side. "It's just ... so much. The archives ... like a maze. I thought I wouldn't make it back for a moment."

"You're better than you think," Neela said encouragingly as she stood up, shaking on ungainly legs at first. She clutched the back of the seat, again warding off Neela and then Pepper with a gesture, though she managed a grateful smile at Xerx's wife. She then indicated the weapons locker.

"Garrison mode was a widely used setting for First Imperium warships during the Imperium Wars," she explained, following Xerx toward the locker, her gait much steadier. "Sometimes heavy combat areas required movement of multiple large troop units, so the ship was designed with... well, the math involved is insane but—"

"Mobola..." Xerx warned.

"I don't know what you'd call it, except for..." Mobola searched the air for the right words, "...some kind of dimensional expansion tech?"

"Come again?" said Salt.

"It makes the ship bigger on the inside than on the outside," Mobola explained, pressing her hand to the scanner at the locker door. It slid open, and a drawer below the weapon racks opened. Inside was what looked like a set of six silver bracelets.

"They're holographic display units," Mobola explained. "They'll display the ship's expanded interior as long as garrison mode is active. They're synchronized with each other as well, so you can keep track of everyone's position. You can plot a course to engineering this way too, since they're connected to the computer. And I suggest you get there soon."

"Okay, we understand," Xerx said impatiently.

"No, you *don't* understand," Mobola said, her voice's pitch making her protest sound more like keening. "The engine is diverting the energy that would have been expended into the garrison mode. We're locked in. That means that there's no way to stop the expansion until we do the reboot."

Var, who had followed the crew alongside Salt and Pepper, let out a curse in his language. "Just how much expansion are we looking at?"

Mobola's voice became so timid, the statement sounded like a question.

"Ultimately, a big explosion." She swallowed hard. "As in, 'eventually we'd never find engineering, even if we had all the time in the world.'"

"Then it looks like we're on a tighter clock than we thought," Xerx said, forcing down the feeling of sickness that began to churn in his stomach. He then turned to Salt, beckoning for him and Pepper to follow.

"It's your lucky day," Xerx said to the older Felyan. "Time to redeem yourself. You and Pepper will be coming with me." He then tossed the pair a MAG rifle and pistol to sort out between them and cast a wry smile at Mobola. "Hopefully, no one will be closing the doors in our faces this time?"

Mobola only managed a sheepish grin of her own.

"Var and Mobola, you two hold down the fort here on the bridge with Neela. Keep us posted on the changes to the ship. Neela, use our genetic IDs and see if you can get a bead on the intruder."

Xerx felt that it should not have taken so long for Neela to calibrate the ship's internal sensors to keep a focused readout on their vitals. In the days of the Old Imperium, he was positive that such a thing had to be instantaneous, especially aboard a warship. Mobola had explained that this was because of the extra lag time from the computer core to the bridge due to the ship's expanding nature. Eventually, the readouts were holding steadily on both their holographic displays and the consoles at the bridge, with multicolored icons representing each crew member. Mobola had patched in a directing path through their bracelets' holo displays that showed the shortest route to engineering, along with a count-down timer that calculated the time to the next garrison mode expansion. To Xerx's dismay, the ship had already gone through two expansions in the time it took to prepare for this mission, costing that much more of their time along with his patience. To make up for lost time, he and his two Felyan crewmates ran most of the way through the ship's interior, following the flashing icon on their displays.

They had only made it through three eerily elongated corridors when it happened. The sound that Pepper made when what could only be described as a wall of crackling electrical current arced its charge into him was something between a cat whose tail had just been stepped on and a jittering howl. The force of the jolt sent him flying back into the bulkhead.

"*Yari!*" Salt cried out and rushed across the corridor to his son, dropping to his knees and sliding the rest of the distance.

It was his sudden drop in stature that proved to be his saving grace.

"Get down!" Xerx screamed to the older Felyan as a high-pitched whine zipped across the corridor. Salt collapsed flat to the ground beside his already prostrate son as a rumbling explosive noise filled the corridor, and a dent appeared in the wall beside the two Felyans.

It had to be a stun round to make a furrow of that size, Xerx observed, but what had fired it? Its ammo had been too big and slow-moving to be a MAG round—but its speed allowed him to pinpoint its source. He returned fire in the opposing direction with the much more lethal ammo of his pistols, suppressing the urge to cringe at starting a gunfight in his own ship. The rounds, thrown by their miniaturized accelerators, punched large holes in the bulkhead on the other side of the corridor, and a cloud of coolant gas spread out from a pierced pipe behind the paneling. Xerx caught a fleeting glimpse of the intruder: a human female. In her right hand was what appeared to be a revolver, an archaic firearms design from Old Earth.

And his scanner's holos hadn't even registered a blip.

Like a spooked rat, she scampered away with near-inhuman speed down a branching corridor. A stream of long, luminous blue hair followed her in her flight. Xerx gave chase, firing again but missing her by inches as she turned down an adjacent corridor. Like a parkour runner on fast-forward, the girl leaped from wall to wall. Xerx kept coming just short of his target with each pull of his trigger until she reached a dead end. That was when she changed the vector with one final leap toward the ceiling, then punched into the paneling above, disappearing into the hole.

For several moments, Xerx could only stare at the makeshift exit, panting, and shaking with barely controlled rage. It was only his wife's voice over the comm that snapped him free of his emotions

"*Kipenzi!*"

"We're okay," Xerx said, his voice unsteady as he backed away from the hole and traced his steps back to where Salt and Pepper were, both still on the ground. A tinge of worry overpowered his anger when he saw the shape of Pepper's clothes: singed on their edges, but when the younger Felyan sat up, despite appearing to be in some amount of pain, Xerx breathed a sigh of relief. Salt was checking over him, though his son, groaning, waved him away.

"Are you sure?" Neela asked, not at all sounding convinced.

"Yeah, we are," Xerx confirmed with more certainty than before.

"What happened? We registered an energy spike and then weapons' fire up here."

"Looks like it was the bitch I ran into outside the hangar back in Pit Town," Xerx said. "She managed to get aboard, *and* she's avoiding the ship's sensors. Damned if I know how, though."

He stepped over to one of the spent rounds that lay below the dent and took it into his hand. It was a solid rubber sphere: not heavy, but at the speed at which it was fired, he imagined that it would have felt like a two-by-four.

"Looks like she's trying to use nonlethal methods," Xerx continued. "She's persistent; I'll give her that." He shifted his gaze to where the arc of electricity that had floored Pepper had come from, and he noticed a now-fried rigging composed of exposed wiring and what he supposed was some kind of sensor array. "She also booby-trapped the hall with a loose power coupling. Laid Pepper out on his ass."

"Is he alright?" The voice was Mobola's.

"I will be," Pepper chimed in. He rose to his feet with his father cautiously standing by. Taking a couple of ungainly steps forward, he flicked his now bushy-looking tail, then shook his head as if to loosen what was inside. His charcoal gray mane waved about like fur from a shaggy dog. "Feels like my insides were turned to jelly, though. You said something about a booby trap?"

"That's what gave you a juicing just now," Xerx said. "The intruder's a guest that Neela and I picked up from Siberna."

"She smelled like that stripey-armed goth bitch we met at the last tournament," Salt remarked with a low growl.

"Artemis?" Xerx said. "You sure about that? As long as I've known her, she's always rocked pink hair."

"Tell that to my nose," the older Felyan replied.

"Probably not wrong there," Xerx said, reconsidering as he again examined the piece of rubber ammo in his fingers, "but non-lethal isn't her thing. Last I heard, she prefers knives."

"Remind me to thank her for her consideration then," was Salt's icy reply.

"Not if I get to her first," Pepper added with equal conviction.

"We're going to have go a bit more slowly, *kidege*," Xerx said, speaking over the comm. "I'm sure we can get to engineering in time, but we don't want to run into more traps. And work a little harder on getting a bead on the intruder. Bitch didn't show up at all when she got the drop on us. She's gotta show up on something."

"Roger that," Neela replied. "Var is still working on it."

"Stay safe," Mobola added, though Xerx was certain that it was addressed more to Pepper than to him.

"I'm sorry to put you guys through this." With a sigh, he holstered his pistols but kept the straps on them loose. "It looks like our mission just got more difficult."

"I'll say," Pepper remarked. There was a telling scowl plastered on his face. "And on that note, you weren't exactly forthcoming with what happened back planetside. One minute Mobola and I are neck-deep in a manifold, and the next, I'm in a world of sirens and we're headed to the bridge to find you spinning tales of intruders. Care to enlighten me before we go running off into even deeper shit?"

"Yeah, that would be helpful," Xerx said, feeling somewhat chagrined at his hurried treatment of the situation. Certain that both of his crewmates were more or less unhurt, he signaled for them to move on. "But I'm afraid we're on a tight schedule, so let's talk while we walk."

"Fair enough," Pepper replied before Xerx began the tale.

SEVEN

"So how exactly did she get on the ship?" Salt asked as the company neared what seemed to be the twentieth corner. Xerx did his best to suppress the growing sense of annoyance he felt at the inconvenient size difference. Even at a brisk pace, they were unable to outrun the next expansion, which left them still on deck 4. Now, according to the display holos at their wrists, the distance they had left to trek until they reached the next elevator had become nearly a quarter mile.

"Damned if I know," Xerx replied, grateful for the conversation. "She wasn't on the Corax. That's for sure. Or else she would've never survived that shit show of a landing."

"Well, I've heard bionics can help people survive exposure to hard vacuum," Pepper said, "in addition to hard impact. If her bones were reinforced, then the landing like you had wouldn't be a problem for her."

"Makes me wonder if I was right about who sent her," Xerx mused aloud.

"What do you mean?"

Xerx heaved a loud sigh. "This one goes back some time ago," he said, "and is more about my cousin Izz."

"Isibar?" Salt said, recalling his full name. "The one who lives on An'Re'Hara?"

Xerx nodded. "He used to be something of a mercenary, but he worked alone. Alliance gave him a mission to Icona, top-secret at the time, but it didn't stay that way after he found those missing kids."

"I remember that!" Pepper pointed at Xerx. "Everyone back home was talking about it. Something about a bunch of hybrid kids going missing, then turning up dead in a lab on Icona, and a Hara'Kya malcontent group being blamed, wasn't it? I was pretty young at the time."

"That you were," Salt said with a soft snort. "Those were bad times; mixed couples were scared shitless. They couldn't pin anything on the group officially until Isibar gave his statement, along with the pictures. The Imperium claimed no knowledge of it, but the malcontents were boned. They were hunted down like a thresher infestation after that. First executions on the homeworld in centuries." A smile of satisfaction sat on his mouth. "I forgot that he was your cousin. So what does that have to do with anything here?"

"What wasn't made public knowledge was the one who was behind it," Xerx said. "Izz did his own investigations and couldn't find much outside of records on Tantagel IX. But with the standoff there, info from some places can be spotty. Her name is Dr. Hayashibara. I guess you could call her a mad scientist. Truth be told, she's just an amoral nutjob. But she's damn smart too. Alliance and the Felyans have been looking for her ever since, but somehow she manages to stay one step ahead of everyone."

"Why would you think she's after you, though?" Pepper asked. "If anything, she'd want revenge on your cousin for ruining her operation on Icona with the malcontents."

"Probably because Felyan Technology is still about half a century ahead of us, and she doesn't want to risk being found out trying to get to him," Xerx said. "And I did say she was smart; she probably knows everything about all of us."

"But that happened over a decade ago," the younger Felyan added.

"From what we've managed to find out, she's got the patience of Job," Xerx replied flatly. "She'll wait years for the perfect opportunity. But really, it's all speculation. For all I know, I could just be paranoid. But my cousin wants me to keep an eye out for her. And I've made a few enemies already, both in the GI and among fellow pirates. This could be anyone."

"Are you *still* worrying about that, love?" Neela's voice popped in over the comm.

"Nah, just thinking out loud," Xerx replied with a smile. "Besides, it's best that our crew knows about this. Also, a good story helps pass the time. But getting back to the former subject, it wouldn't surprise me if this guest of ours is enhanced in some pretty special ways." A vision of the girl's face, but with shorter, pink hair, once again intruded into his thoughts as he spoke. "She does remind me of Artemis, though, now that you guys mentioned it."

"She enhanced too?" Pepper asked.

"I heard a few things," Xerx replied, recalling the hearsay from the regulars back at the Greasy Gear, "like how she moves. She took a glass to the face from Radic once at the Gear. 'Never seen anyone move so fast,' they said. She put an ice pick through the table—via his hand. Not a mark on her."

The younger Felyan made a low, elongated curse in his language, while his father gave a hastily made holy gesture.

"She one of these enemies you mentioned?" Salt inquired.

"Who in the GI doesn't have a grudge against someone?" Xerx said with a dismissive wave. "But you know me; I usually settle grudges in the arena. 'Sides, Arty's someone you don't want to hold a grudge against."

"Why's that?" Pepper asked.

"Aside from the business of leaving an ice pick in a man's hand?" Salt replied incredulously. "I'm thinking she'd settle any grudge with you before you would."

"And if her performance in the tourneys is any indication of how she can fight outside a Gestalt," Xerx added, "you damn well know it wouldn't end in your favor."

As the group approached what appeared to be the final corner that would lead to the elevator, Xerx paused and signaled his two Felyan partners. Pressing himself against the corner, he snuck a peek around its edge. Down the corridor appeared to be a straight shot to the elevator door. Perhaps it was only the fact that he'd watched too many Old Earth horror movies as a kid, but the apparent ease of this situation set off a distinct sense of dread in the back of his mind.

"Anyone else think this is a trap?" Pepper said, his voice tense.

"Well, if it wasn't before, it might be now, with the noise you're making," the older Felyan remarked with some irritation.

Pepper hissed. "What are you talking about? We were just making enough noise to wake the—" Suddenly, he froze, wide-eyed. "Wait. Something doesn't smell right."

"*Kipenzi*," Neela's voice broke into their comm units instead of the ship's intercom. "A blip appeared on our monitors ... and then disappeared."

"A ... blip?" Xerx said, his voice flat.

"Unauthorized DNA." Mobola's reply was uncharacteristically terse. "Captain, there's something there with you."

Both Felyans, hearing the conversation, frowned.

"She's right behind us, isn't she, dad?" Pepper asked, without looking away from his position beside his father.

"That's a safe bet, son," was Salt's morose reply.

"Ain't nothing 'safe' about this bitch," Xerx said, taking a cue from his crewmates. Without looking back, he fired a single shot behind him, angling it to pass above his crewmates' heads. As expected, the MAG round hit only air, but a movement in his peripheral vision told him all he needed. He struck out with his fist, hitting the solid yet slightly pliant contours of flesh, the impact and ensuing grunt indicating that he had struck a ribcage. He ducked despite seeing nothing, but he then heard the movement of air above indicating that he'd avoided a retaliatory blow. Rotating the pistol in his hand and turning it into a useful bludgeon, he swung for a consecutive strike, but his loaded fist only passed through air. Before he could get his bearings, a sharp blow crackled pain across his upper back like an explosive. Not having braced for the impact, Xerx heaved a coughing grunt before another blow, this time across his face, destroyed all sense of direction. Stars burst behind his eyes as his face connected with a nearby bulkhead, its cold contours sliding against his bruised skin as his legs gave out. Everything about him was now occurring in double vision and garbled echoes. It was only the cries of his crewmates that prevented him from giving completely into the darkness that licked at the edges of his vision.

Defiantly, Xerx crawled to his hands and knees as echoes solidified into discernible sounds, and his vision began to clear. He caught sight of the blue-haired girl, now dragging Pepper by the neck with something that resembled a rope. It was too thick to be any kind of garrote; in fact, if he hadn't known any better, he would have sworn it had been made from her hair, as its fibers matched the color of her long, blue locks. It was looped across the younger Felyan's neck, its slackened end held in her left hand. Salt charged at her from the left, his rifle raised, and Xerx, still winded and in pain, could only watch as, with her free hand, the girl struck the older Felyan in the chest with her open palm. Salt careened into the opposite bulkhead, leaving a dent in the metal and carbon fiber paneling.

Xerx, fighting against pain, gritted his teeth and braced himself against the wall. He propped his right shoulder securely against it as his hand sought the gun holster at his hip. Buoyed by a combination of fear and anger, he set his jaw and powered through his remaining disorientation, drawing the weapon and taking aim at the girl's forehead, thankful at how Salt's ill-conceived strategy had at least distracted her.

The shot missed its mark by mere inches, grazing the left side of her head and tearing her ear in two. The girl let out a yelp and fell back, sprawling onto the floor and dropping the younger Felyan in the process. Xerx ran on instinct, stumbling forward and catching Pepper, who fell to the floor, gasping.

"I'm okay!" he managed to wheeze. "Dad..."

"On it," Xerx said, eyeing the gray-haired Felyan, who lay propped up against the dented wall, dazed as he had been only moments ago. Xerx gestured to the elevator door across the hall. "Move your ass."

As Pepper scrambled down the hall, Xerx leaped over to Salt's side, making sure there was no obvious injury before hoisting his crewmate onto his shoulder. Even now, he could see the girl was starting to move, the flesh of her damaged ear knitting back together with frightening speed. If she had the same kind of self-repair nanos as her twin, even a shot to the head wouldn't be enough to put her down permanently.

"Tell someone to put a cap on the *riss*, Cap'n ..." Salt grumbled as Xerx secured the Felyan's arm about his neck and his own arm about his waist.

"You might want it to numb the pain after the hurt that girl laid on you," Xerx said, following Pepper toward the elevator door. He cursed under his breath at the sight of the discarded rifle, which there wasn't enough time to reach.

"And give me a week-long case of wood," Salt replied, dazedly. "Thanks, but unless I'm at a pleasure house, I'll just take a nice bottle of Sepra Gold."

"I'm surprised you couldn't smell her ... coming...," Xerx said, his voice trailing off as he noticed something odd about the hallway. "What the hell?"

He glanced behind him to find the girl now standing upright but with a look as confused as his own. Then he realized why. They had been standing much closer only moments ago, but now it seemed as though, without having even budged, she had moved a full meter away.

"Shit," he mumbled as he glanced at his holo readout. The counter had reached zero and was resetting. Right on time, Mobola's voice crackled in over the comm.

"Captain, the ship's undergoing another expansion."

"Thank you, Captain Obvious," Xerx muttered at a volume that he hoped she couldn't hear.

"My readouts say you stopped moving. Time is running out."

"Tell me something I don't know," Xerx snapped back, trying to pick up his already greatly slowed pace. "Our guest sidetracked us again. Pepper's okay, but Salt got the stupid knocked back into him."

"Is she still there?" Neela said.

"She just gave my face a close encounter with a wall," Xerx replied, the side of his head still throbbing from its recent abuse.

"Captain, we've got problems," Salt said as Xerx noticed Pepper put forth a burst of speed and arrive at the door, sliding like a baseball player next to the panel. He was frantically pressing the call button as the older Felyan gestured back the way they'd come. "She's coming after us!"

"Of course she is!" Xerx said, his tone rife with sarcastic enthusiasm. "How fast?"

"Fast."

Xerx paused and drew his pistol. He had been prepared to pivot around and try his luck at targeting their guest, but Salt stopped him. "No, keep going," he said, reaching out with his hand. "Give the gun to me."

Xerx passed the weapon to Salt and pressed forward, glancing back behind him only once before his crewmate started firing. It appeared that the girl was still not at one hundred percent, her movements were not fully coordinated as she closed the distance between them in the rapidly extending hallway with a brisk and slightly ungainly canter. Xerx heard the shots ring out amidst the older Felyan's frustrated snarls and the hiss of broken pipes as the accelerated rounds pierced the walls. He hadn't held out much hope of him nailing her; he was nowhere near as proficient with small firearms and was hardly in any condition to handle one; still, there was a chance that he could get lucky. But this luck was sadly not in the cards.

"She's moving too damn fast," Salt complained, as ahead, Xerx noticed Pepper shaking free of his momentary panic and drawing his own pistol to make well-placed covering fire. Xerx put forth one last effort and pressed forward the rest of the way, his speed still hampered to a half-jog. At last, he fell to one knee beside the younger Felyan, panting.

"Elevator's taking a lot longer to get here," Pepper said, firing once again. Xerx felt Salt roll off his back and brace himself on the bulkhead beside the door, freeing him to turn around and make a clear shot with his remaining pistol.

Neither father nor son, however, mentioned just how much ground she'd covered. In spite of their suppression fire, the girl managed to leap forward now with far more confident strides, bursting through the searing walls of steam in the hallway and deftly avoiding the barrage of MAG rounds. Breathing deeply, Xerx quietly drew his spare pistol. He lined up his shots, pulling the trigger in quick succession, finally finding that elusive luck. Five rounds slammed into her chest and legs, sending her sprawling again to the ground and splattering blood on the nearby walls, floor, and ceiling.

With a high-pitched chime, the elevator door at last opened.

SEVEN

"Inside, now!" Xerx shouted as Pepper grabbed his father. "Move your asses!"

As if she had not been plugged with ammo only a moment before, the girl sprang to her feet. She charged forward, covering the remaining distance to the elevator door in less than two seconds. Xerx scrambled backwards into the elevator car, and crouching on his haunches, he drew his knife. The moment she clutched at the sides of the doorway, he sprang forward, plunging the blade solidly into her gut. He braced himself in the doorway, then staggered back as the girl tumbled with a pained shriek, yanking the knife from her abdomen. He watched as blood spilled out of the wound and ducked as the girl tossed the blade back toward him, wedging it into the back of the elevator car as the doors sealed shut.

EIGHT

As the elevator began its descent, Xerx collapsed against the wall, feeling the blood thrumming in his regret-filled head. Wearily, he glanced to his left at the two beleaguered Felyans. Salt, not yet having recovered fully from the wallop he'd received only moments ago, leaned forward, baring his teeth in a groaning rictus as he cradled his head in his hand. His tail sat twitching limply on the floor beside him.

Xerx opened his mouth, ready to ask Salt if he would be all right, but Pepper asked first.

"I sure hope so," the older Felyan answered his son. "The room stopped spinning, but it hurts to breathe." A second later, he barked out a sharp cry, and his son jerked his hands back. "Dammit, Yari! Warn me when you're going to do that!"

"Broken rib, isn't it?" Xerx asked, seeing Pepper kneeling beside his father and reaching for his injured side yet again while the older Felyan swatted his hands away.

"I'm not a doctor, but I'll bet credits to crap that the answer would be yes," Pepper replied.

"With how hard that bitch threw him, I'm only thankful he doesn't have a broken spine," Xerx added then switched his attention to the bracelet's holos. "I wonder how much longer we have 'til we reach the engine room?"

He brought the device's display, but all it seemed to show was the elevator shaft: a seemingly endless line with the blinking green icons indicating their life signs descending an equally endless series of empty decks.

"Just how big *is* this ship now?" Xerx turned and noticed Salt staring agape at the readouts on his bracelet.

"By now, the interior has grown to four times its original size," Neela said, answering the rhetorical question over the comm.

"We're looking at about ten minutes between expansions," Mobola added. "At this rate, you have about two more expansions before getting to the engine room. If you don't get there by then, getting there in time will be impossible."

Xerx stood and stretched, checking the ammo clip of his MAG pistol and sighing. "No pressure," he muttered. "But we'd have been there by now, if it hadn't been for that—"

Xerx noticed it, mid-sentence: the ominous red flash of the intruder in the readouts, appearing for barely a second, then vanishing, its movements rapid in its descending pursuit down the shaft. Cursing in a harsh whisper, Xerx aimed up with his pistols, taking a rooted stance.

"Gonna have to finish this later, *kipenzi*," Xerx said as he saw Pepper rising slowly to his feet, the grip on his pistol tightening, his tail swishing anxiously back and forth.

"Dad, stay down," the younger Felyan warned his father. Xerx noticed him glancing furtively at his own bracelet's readouts. "She's fast," he observed. You think she's freefalling?"

"She's fucking crazy if she is," Xerx replied, "but on the bright side, if she kills us, it's better than dying in a pulsar."

"Not funny," he heard Salt say with another groan.

"For once we agree," Pepper added.

"What sucks is the waiting," Xerx said, holding his aim. "At that speed, she should be here by now."

"I know," Pepper said. "It's like in a movie—"

A loud *thump* from above shattered the conversation. Xerx was at first hesitant to fire until a cacophony of crunching sounds shrieked into the former silence. As the lights in the elevator flashed and went out and the dim emergency lights at the edges of the walls remained, he opened fire.

What fresh hell is this? Xerx thought, as a shower of sparks and debris cascaded around his head. *Is she not up there?* Surely he had to have hit something. He jumped back from the debris of the pulverized elevator ceiling as a twisted knot of steel sliced through the air, creating a small rip in his jacket. Darkness loomed within the hole that was opening above. Xerx wasted no time, firing again into the hole, but the gloom within stymied any chances of a clear shot. His Felyan companions, however, were not so hampered. In unison, father and son cursed in their native tongue as the darkness was shattered, if only for a split second with each shot from Pepper's gun, highlighting the nightmarish form of the relentless blue-haired girl, who now hovered above Xerx. As he combined his firepower with his crewmate, each flash showed her in a different position, her moves like a professional dancer in a strobe light as she dodged their shots.

Xerx's sense of fear redoubled as the girl took advantage of a slight lull in the barrage to dive into the furrow. With the same terrifying speed that she'd displayed each encounter, her hands fired downward and seized his wrists with vice-like strength. He yelped as a surge of pain fired through his wrists in her crushing grip, his pistol clattering to the floor as he was hoisted upward like a sack of potatoes.

Before her unnatural strength could clear the ragged hole in the ceiling, a second pressure enveloped his calves, then pulled him down with the same urgency, if not equal force. But it seemed to be enough to take the girl by surprise. The strength of her grip faltered, but her determination did not. Xerx felt like the rope in a tug-of-war as two opposing forces fought for control of him. He glanced down, toward the sight of Pepper, the charcoal gray-haired Felyan heaving with all his might, his arms wrapped firmly about his calves, but still holding his gun, his clenched teeth showing their slightly more pronounced canines as he fought desperately against her superior grip. All the while, Xerx felt ever more like a hapless victim about to be broken on the rack.

"She's ... too ... strong!" Pepper grunted as the strength of his pull faltered. Xerx's mind raced; God only knew this crazy woman's plans.

"Shoot her!" Xerx snarled through his clenched teeth.

"I might hit you!" Pepper protested.

"You can't hold on forever!" Xerx shouted back. "She's too strong, and you know it; shoot her! That's an order!"

As he watched Pepper wrestle with his desire to free him and his reticence at firing at such a narrow target, it dawned upon Xerx that though his wrists were in the girl's unbreakable grasp, her wrists were free: a fortuitous situation. He wrapped his hands about her much narrower arms and dug his fingers into the median nerves, pushing down with all of his might.

The girl let out a wail of pain making Xerx instantly grateful that she possessed the same pressure points as any other human— and at the same time regretful that this gave Pepper more leverage than he needed. Her grip faltered, though not enough to make her let go. But the sudden pain seemed enough to ruin her sense of balance and send her tumbling down through the hole and into the elevator. Xerx landed painfully on his back, slightly winded, but otherwise no more hurt than before.

He tried to roll away and leap to his feet, but the girl was quicker, lashing out with well-trained limbs and landing a punch to his face that at once destroyed his balance and sent him sliding into the wall. It did not land as smartly as he'd expected, and he shook away his momentary double-vision to see that the girl was no worse off than he was. Having righted herself after her fall, she was now facing Pepper. His pistol lay unclaimed on the floor, not but three feet from him, and the younger Felyan was gingerly gripping his wrist, growling in a manner that Xerx had only heard once from Var right before a bar fight that banned him from the Greasy Gear for three months.

Seemingly not hurt enough, Pepper launched himself at the girl, the tapered claws of his uninjured hand reaching for her face. The girl, however, dodged him as deftly as she'd avoided their volley of MAG rounds. Using his momentum against him, she grabbed his shirt and belt, tossing him full force into the opposite wall where he fell into a motionless heap.

Feeling the sensation creep back into his hands after his tug-of-war, Xerx slid his foot out and dragged the pistol his way. Kicking it into the air, he grabbed the weapon in his right hand, removed the knife he'd pried from the elevator wall and sheathed in the holster at his belt. Shoving down his fear as the girl turned toward him, he stood up on ungainly legs, aiming for her head. To his surprise, she held her ground, seemingly waiting for him to make the first move. He stole a glance at Pepper, who seemed out cold, and then at Salt, who sat against the wall, a helpless observer.

He instantly regretted his loss of focus.

The girl struck with precision speed, her fist flying forward, which Xerx parried and retaliated with a thrust from his knife at her neck, which she parried with a sweeping upward strike. He fired two shots, and she became a blur as she dodged the MAG rounds, a well-placed palm strike sending a numbing pain down his wrist that paralyzed his firing hand. Having been struck with a blow that felt more like a baseball bat than a limb, the weapon was reintroduced to the ground. Again, her iron grip came down upon his wrist. Quick as a serpent's strike, Xerx used his uninjured hand to catch the wrist of her opposite arm in his grip, changing the fight into a wrestling match.

EIGHT

It was a fight he had no chance of winning, as the girl asserted her prodigious strength and leverage, tossing him into the wall with a much crueler force than she'd used against Pepper. The blow knocked the wind out of him and sent a burst of stars flashing in his field of view. Gasping for air, Xerx curled into a fetal ball, seeing his discarded knife through tear-blurred vision hopelessly out of reach. He nearly retched from the sudden loss of oxygen until his lungs at last inflated, flooding him with blessed air. Still, pain radiated throughout his back from the blow, and his vision still had not cleared. All that was left was the grim realization that he wasn't getting up anytime soon.

"Why do you resist?"

The girl's voice came from directly above him now. The closest things he could see were her feet, clad in the reinforced footgear that was part of her form-fitting black Imperial uniform.

"Who ... the fuck ... sent you?" Xerx quavered.

"You'll find out soon enough," the girl replied. "Now answer my question."

"My crew ... needs me."

"They're no longer your concern." The girl's voice was passive, almost emotionless.

"Then you've sentenced us to death," Xerx answered.

He felt her hands grab him by the lapels of his jacket. Heaven help her if she tore it even more.

"The fault is yours. You could've just come with me on Siberna."

"You'll have to kill me first, then."

"Not in the cards."

Xerx's vision cleared just enough to see her raise her hand. A long, silver needle appeared to form from the tip of her index finger. But then, through tear-filled vision, he also became aware of a figure that hovered shakily behind her. Was its arm raised? No, that seemed too long for an arm. Nevertheless, it was poised for a strike that was quickly delivered. It struck home with near-deadly force, and the girl instantly slumped to the ground, taking Xerx with her. Still reeling from her prior blow, Xerx picked himself painfully up from the floor, his body a mass of bruises. His vision cleared, revealing Salt standing directly behind the spot where the girl now lay, his discarded pistol in hand, stained with blood.

"You okay, Captain?" Salt asked, grabbing Xerx by the hand—thankfully the uninjured one—and helping him to stand. His legs still unsure and his body still wracked with pain, Xerx rose to his feet, propping himself against the dented wall of the elevator to steady himself.

"I'll live," Xerx said and nodded toward Pepper. "Didn't want to risk shooting me, huh?"

Salt shook his head. "I think my son had the right idea, even though you ordered him to shoot. Bullets didn't seem to work on that bitch, so I figured I'd smack her upside the head and see how that worked out."

"Well, it worked," Xerx remarked, nodding toward the girl's unconscious form. "She doesn't look like she'll be getting up for a while." He then nodded at Pepper. "Go see about your son."

"What about her?" Salt asked, kicking the girl for good measure.

Xerx stood over the girl's motionless form, having picked up his pistol. Without hesitation, he fired two shots at her skull. But even the finality of these did not set him at ease.

"I don't want to press our luck, as fast as she recovers," Xerx said.

"You just double-tapped her, Captain," Salt protested. "She's not gonna get any deader."

"Yeah, and I shot her several times in the chest and ran her through the gut with a knife," Xerx said, "so pardon me if I'm not totally convinced. We'll stop the elevator and drop her off on one of those expanded decks. The distance between us will at least give me some peace of mind."

"You're pacing," Var observed from his console.

"Thank you; I'm quite aware," Neela replied impatiently. She knew her husband had a reputation for surviving the most harrowing situations, but the problem was that these situations had a habit of *always* popping up, and at the worst times. His comm had gone silent, and the last she had heard over it, it sounded like some kind of fight—one that neither he nor their crewmates seemed to be winning.

A gasp from Mobola broke her chain of dark ruminations.

"Is something wrong?" she asked, moving away from the rut she was threatening to wear into the floor and coming to Mobola's side. She glanced at the hologram readouts, the LIDAR grid showing multiple contacts. Var's massive form soon towered behind them both. A rumble from the taciturn *Hara'kya* Felyan betrayed the worry that was quite mutual.

"Is that what I think it is?" Neela asked.

Mobola nodded. "Multiple ships on approach and at high speed. And... Oh, no."

Neela knew a hostile I.F.F. signal when she saw it. And the insignias told all.

"Well, pirates are good, right?" Var said. "Our captain's from Rhoma, after all."

"Not all pirates are our friends," Neela admonished the hairy Felyan hulk. She enhanced the image of one of the insignias: a skull with double rings but with a snake running through a single eye socket.

"They're pirates, alright," Mobola said with morbid finality, "just the wrong kind."

NINE

"This was the last job," Four had told her.

It was *always* the "last job."

It had been the "last job" for fifteen years.

"Ronin to Shogun," she said into her comm implant, knowing how she'd just defied Four's orders to keep radio silence. "Mission SNAFU, request extraction."

A sour, mocking smile creased the edges of Nemesis' mouth at the responding void of silence.

"Any way the wind blows," she said, and that was exactly how it felt. Four's plans seemed to change with the wind, and she'd taken to saying the words as a means of voicing her disapproval. She had gone along with those plans for a long time now, and over that time, her feelings for him had grown into a deep love. Perhaps, then, this was what love drove one to do: always completing that "one last job," no questions, no protest, just getting it done regardless of the cost.

But this time, she had to admit that this was pushing it. She had absolute faith in her ability to achieve her objective: capture and retrieve the cousin of the pirate king, but she would be lying if she hadn't harbored reservations against going after such a target. The last thing she wanted to be was a catalyst for an interstellar war.

And where the hell was she?

"Ronin to Shogun; come in. Mission SNAFU, extraction requested."

Nemesis' mounting dismay exacerbated her already throbbing head, but the nanites did their work, sealing the wound and repairing the remainder of the damage from both the bludgeon and the two MAG rounds as though they had never been there. The pain would be merely residual, a psychological after-effect that even the tiny machines in her cells couldn't block. Absently, she rubbed her head as she ambled through the seemingly endless hallway. Identifying a maintenance hatch, she opened it and began climbing through the service shafts as the ship's interior continued to shift around her.

Minute by minute, she found herself awakening to the unthinkable possibility that she had been stranded in enemy territory, part of an operation that was beyond saving. A sharp ghost of pain shot through her gut at the very real fear that she might never see Four again.

Exiting the service tunnel, Nemesis perched on the lip of the elevator shaft once more. She considered another suicide dive in an attempt to catch up with her quarry, but she thought better of it, as she'd burned out her grav chutes in the previous jump. Her nanites could repair her body, but even they had limits.

She eventually returned to the main decks, their unending, monotonous corridors creating an illusion she'd been placed between two mirrors and was caught forever as part of their endless series of mutual reflections. Anxiety began to replace despair, asserting its coldness into her belly. She was now, undeniably, lost … and so was the mission.

"Oh, *kidege*, thank God you made it!" Xerx could detect a note of unrelated tension in Neela's voice over the comm as he and his crew exited the damaged elevator car. "We don't have much time left."

"Thank God indeed," he replied. "But what about you?"

"Outside of the usual, there is a ... complication on my end."

He hated being right.

"What kind of 'complication'?" Xerx exchanged glances with his crewmates, their expressions sharing the same note of unease at her news.

"Switch to a private channel," Neela said. "I don't want everyone to worry."

"We're already worried," Xerx said, but he switched over regardless. He lowered his voice to a more confidential tone. "What's the problem?"

"We may have company. Lots of it."

"Raiders?"

"Looks that way."

"Shit."

"They're moving in and out of the hyperspace energy streams, so they're hard to track, but we're definitely being followed," Neela said.

"Well, one thing at a time," Xerx replied. "On the bright side, if we get blown to bits colliding with a pulsar, there won't be much left for them to steal."

"We are seriously going to have to work on your comedic timing," his wife said flatly.

"As I said, *kipenzi*, one thing at a time."

Xerx wasted no time taking point. Still shaken by their recent encounter with the blue-haired intruder and not willing to take chances, he led his Felyan crewmates into the corridor, hands poised on his MAG pistols' respective triggers. The fact that they had to move quickly with this ever-present danger in mind, and against a steadily ticking clock, was nerve-wracking. Salt had recovered enough from his injury to walk unaided, but the blow he'd suffered in the elevator had rung his bell thoroughly enough to stymie his pace considerably.

"And I thought the ship was too damn big before," the older Felyan muttered, grasping hold of a bulkhead, panting and grasping his knees as he leaned forward. It was the third time he had called for a moment to rest, much to Xerx's frustration. His tail was twitching as if it were that of a dying lizard. "I've half a mind to have you guys leave me behind and let the blue-haired bitch find me."

"Not gonna happen, Dad," Pepper said and hurried to his father's side, taking his arm over his shoulder. "And I sure as hell ain't gonna have you die on me."

Salt chuckled as he kept the pace of his son, buoyed by his added strength. "Well, I guess I wouldn't want the captain to die on my watch... lose his title hopes ..."

"Being dead won't be a problem," Xerx fired back with a playful glance. "It's been won by a dead guy before."

"Wow, aren't we a bright and sunny bunch," Pepper chimed in.

"Hey, I'm ready to live until my tail is bent into a knot," Salt replied

"Keep that optimism," Xerx said. "We're gonna need it."

The two Felyans cast a confused glance his way, but Xerx didn't have the heart to tell them about what his wife had said over the comm. Still, the brief conversation had been playing itself on repeat in his mind ever since—as if he didn't have enough to worry about; life was just pissing on him today without the common courtesy of calling it rain. If they truly were Raiders, it wasn't surprising that the bridge crew was having trouble tracking them. They masked themselves outside of the energy streams of hyperspace corridors, lying in wait for slow-moving ships, homing in on emergency broadcasts, then striking hard and fast. No doubt Neela had sent out an SOS, but it was the worst kind of luck that they'd caught the attention of Raiders now, of all times.

It felt like they had traveled a mile—and Xerx supposed it most likely *had* been a mile of corridor that they had passed through—when, like three parched travelers searching for a mythical oasis, they began to hear the familiar thrumming of the tesseract drive.

"Thank the Creator!" he heard Pepper say as they quickened their pace. "She's sounding pretty rough, though."

"What do you mean?" Xerx asked. Starship specs were not his forte; the heartbeat-like hum of one drive sounded the same as another to him, but the young Felyan held a special talent for diagnosing engine problems by sound alone, even with Gestalt systems.

"Sounds wrong, all wrong," Pepper replied with a disquieting level of alarm. "It's like a choir all singing out of tune."

"Good thing we have the voice coach with us then," Xerx said, reaching the massively shielded entry hatch. There was a patchwork of caution symbols affixed to its steel surface: some common warnings among symbols whose meanings had been lost in the centuries of chaos after the Imperium Wars. He punched in the code and stood back with Salt and Pepper as the hatch swung open at a ponderous pace. Briefly, he checked the timer on his bracelet.

Not even thirty minutes. Not even he could fight against the pit in his stomach.

"We're cutting it down to the wire, people," he said, keeping his voice even while, at the same time, wishing that the A.I. systems that governed the ship knew how to open the door faster. "Let's get this thing done."

"You might find yourself a bit out of your league here, Captain," Pepper said, taking the lead. "You haven't been down here much. Mobola and I had to know this place like I know my own tail."

"You probably got the chance to know *her* tail pretty good down here," Salt interjected, against which his son retorted with the deepest, most aggressive-sounding growl that Xerx had ever heard from him.

"Dad, I told you, we never—!" he began, but Xerx had had his absolute fill of their bickering.

"Not the damn time for that!" he barked, startling both father and son to silence as they passed through the engineering section's entranceway. The consecutive hallway that now stood before them with its grated floor and incomprehensible tangle of conduits beneath was mercifully short.

"Seems the garrison mode effect didn't alter this part of the ship," Salt remarked.

"It's an energy source," Pepper said as they passed the hatches and repeated series of emergency bulkheads under the dimmer light. "I doubt it would take well to dimensional splicing."

"Barely understood what you said," Xerx admitted, "but it sounds bad."

"Not half as bad as what'll happen to us if we don't get the engine fixed," the younger Felyan said as they arrived at the entrance hatch to the graviton siphon. Xerx was good with repairs on the scale of a Gestalt, but now, he conceded their fates to the hands of the resident tech genius.

He checked his timer. Twenty-five minutes.

The graviton siphon lay beyond the hallway, a monstrous piece of machinery from a bygone age, yet distinctively anachronistic in design. With the exception of the more numerous sets of tubing that connected it to conduits high above, it was an almost perfect replica of the old internal combustion engines he'd seen in library records and the antique collections of people with more money than sense. These extravagantly wealthy individuals owned extremely rare vintage cars from Old Earth with the archaic engines that had been snuck on board the arks on the original colonists' passage. It was amusing how someone had designed starfaring technology in their image.

Behind the siphon lay the hyperdrive unit, modeled in a fashion to an engine part called the "transmission" to Xerx's recollection. It thrummed with a rhythm that he could now feel in his skull. Aside from this, however, nothing seemed amiss, but Pepper's brow was furrowed with concern. He followed his crewmate as the younger Felyan ran over to a segment of paneling on the manifold, which appeared to have been hastily covered over its moorings, and slid it out of place.

"Looks like the seals held," he said as he lowered himself to all fours. He then removed a flashlight from one of the pouches in his cargo pants and proceeded to slide into the open aperture. It appeared wide enough for a person his size, tail and all, with room to spare, but he left his legs sticking out prominently.

"Shit, this is cramped," he muttered as he busied himself with whatever had been left undone within the space. "I forget how tiny Mobola is."

"What were you doing?" Xerx asked.

"I was running a power relay check at one of the terminals while Mobola was in this crawlspace," Pepper replied. "She was interfaced with the systems when you gave the order to jump to hyperspace. I tugged her away and slammed the cover over it all before we bolted."

"Enough about the human girl," Salt said impatiently. "Can you fix it? And how long will it take?"

"I'm not sure what part of the hyperdrive she was working on exactly," Pepper replied. "And she has those things that come out of the back of her hands, like the captain's lifemate. They feed data to her." He stuck his hand out of the hole and made a gesture, pointing to the right, then left. "Speaking of terminals, here should be a tablet on one of them. I have a good idea of what happened... I think."

"You *think*?" Salt raised an eyebrow.

"Tablet, please!" Pepper gesticulated impatiently as his tail twitched. Xerx quickly located the device atop the controls of a nearby terminal and placed it into Pepper's open hand, which quickly disappeared back into the hole.

"This isn't like reconnecting circuits on a Gestalt," he said. "And the damn thing is switched on, so I don't want to go fiddling around with too much—" He paused mid-sentence, then hissed out a Felyan curse. "Mobola, you there?"

"Um, yes?" Mobola's comm reply came, soft and nervous-sounding, as usual.

"What were you working on when we had to evacuate engineering?"

There was a pause followed by a very confused-sounding response. "The ...uh, distributor?"

"I know that, *en'li*, but can you be a little more specific?"

Another pause, and Xerx could see Pepper tapping his shoes together with the same impatience that he felt. He checked the timer. Twenty minutes.

"No pressure, 'kay? It's only our lives at stake."

"Please, I'm just... I'm trying to recall it." The distress in Mobola's already shaky voice ratcheted considerably higher. "It... it was the relays on the spatial flux calibrators. Segment M-2905."

"M-2905..." There was a shuffling sound as Pepper's tail twitched. "'Kay, found it." Yet another pause. "And ... no relays."

"That's because I never got the chance to put them back in." There was a trace of hurt in the girl's voice. "You dragged me out an—"

"Focus, please," Pepper said with audibly strained patience. "You can chew me out about it later. Okay, I found the relays. They're lying here on the ground where you left them. How do we put them in?"

Mobola's response, even over the comm was so soft as to barely even be heard.

"You... you have to turn the engine off."

"Fuck," Salt muttered.

"Likewise," Xerx added flatly.

Pepper fired a sternly pointed finger from the hole, sweeping back and forth.

"Not helping, you two!" he growled. "Look, one of you make yourselves useful. There will be three toggle switches on the terminal where you found the tablet. Could one of you go there and wait for a sec?"

Xerx returned to the terminal and located the three toggles, each marked with a different color light. "The ones with the red, gray, and blue lights?" he called out to Pepper.

"Yeah, that's it," Pepper said. "Now, I'm gonna have to put in the relays in a certain order. The second I announce the ones that are in, I need you to flip the corresponding toggle. Red for red, gray for gray, blue for blue. Got it?"

"Yeah." Xerx licked away the sweat that had begun to form on his upper lip. "Matching colors."

"Just don't get it wrong," Pepper said. "We only get one shot at this."

"Why? What happens if I get it wrong?" Xerx said.

"They'll balance out the rate of spatial collapse as power is being rerouted," Pepper replied. "If that doesn't happen... well, you ever heat up an empty can with a blowtorch, then throw it in cold water?"

Xerx swallowed. "Okay. Wrong order, bad," he said. "No pressure. Let's do it."

He looked over at Salt, who was shaking his head.

"A centuries-old warship and regulating power flow is as simple as screwing in a few relays and pushing some buttons," the older Felyan muttered.

"It's better than threading a million wires," Xerx remarked, shrugging his shoulders.

"There has to be another way," Mobola interjected, sounding more desperate than Xerx had ever heard her.

"Look, *en'li*," Pepper said with an astoundingly saint-like calm, "we don't have a choice. We're gonna have to do this while the engine's running. Is there anything you can tell me about it?"

"Um... don't do it?"

"Okay, that would've been funny if our collective asses weren't on the line." Xerx could tell that the Felyan had tried his best to hold back a sardonic tone, which might have flustered the younger tech into becoming impossible to work with. "But seriously, is there anything we should know about the order of the relays that I don't already know?"

"But it could—"

Pepper heaved a frustrated sigh, shutting off Mobola's protest. "If you have a better way, I'm all ears. If not, then tell me what order."

Faintly, Xerx heard Neela over the comm speaking something to Mobola in a reassuring tone that he couldn't make out. Whatever it was, however, it seemed to have a positive effect on the younger girl because her instructions were now spoken with a great deal more confidence.

"The best way would be the red relay, then gray, then blue," she said and then followed it with a distressed addendum. "But it may end up feeding too much power into the siphon! If that happens, we'll—"

"Gonna have to cross that bridge when we come to it." Pepper made his interjection with false nonchalance, to which Mobola replied in a significantly less carefree quaver.

"Please don't come to it."

Xerx shared the sentiment as he waited for the first result.

"Okay, red's in," Pepper said a moment later. Xerx flipped the toggle next to the red light. There was a long pause after. Still alive.

Xerx checked his timer. Five minutes.

"Where the hell did the time go?" he muttered in combined horror and fascination.

Suddenly, the thrumming of the hyperdrive crescendoed two entire octaves. Xerx's heart pounded in his chest, but he refrained from ordering the Felyan to stop. It was either take a trip into the heart of a pulsar or die from what would most likely be an explosion. While neither way was preferable, both would be thankfully swift. But if this was truly the end, his only regret was that he could not be with Neela for it.

"Gray's in," Pepper said soon after the crescendo ended. Xerx flipped the gray switch and the thrumming increased in speed to where he could now feel it in his teeth.

"Neela," Xerx murmured into his comm. "I just want you to know that if this doesn't work ... I love you."

There was a pause. His wife's response came in a whisper. "I love you, *kipenzi*."

Moment of truth, Xerx thought, now feeling better. *Or the moment to meet our maker, perhaps?*

"Blue ... is ... in!" Pepper said.

Eyes squeezed shut, Xerx flipped the blue toggle.

The silence from the engine fell on Xerx like another sneak attack from the blue-haired girl. Everything, in fact, seemed to stop in that selfsame moment of pristine, interstitial quiescence.

He checked his timer. Five seconds. Was time going by faster?

In a sensation that was at once jarring, beyond bizarre, and thankfully brief, Xerx felt as if he were air being compressed into an accordion. It ended just as quickly as it began, and Xerx looked around. Nothing had changed. He began to figure that he was at least alive. Or at least he hoped he was.

His ears popped uncomfortably, leaving him slightly dizzy. He looked at Salt, who had loosened his nervous grip on his tail, which he had been nearly twisting apart in his hands.

Slowly, Pepper squirmed out of the hole in the manifold and replaced the paneling.

"Well, don't just leave us in suspense," Xerx said anxiously as the younger Felyan stood and dusted himself off. "I gotta hear the news; did we do it?"

"Either that or the afterlife is a really boring place," Pepper said with a shrug. He glanced back at the combination monolith that was the hyperdrive and siphon. He then shifted his gaze to the front of his cargo pants, at which point he exhaled with a relaxed grin. "Oh, good. I didn't piss myself after all."

"I nearly did that for you," Xerx said and clapped Pepper on the back, followed quickly by Salt. Both he and the older Felyan laughed in spite of themselves.

"So why'd the engines shut off?" Xerx asked. "It sounded so abrupt; is there anything wrong?"

"Nothing's wrong, Captain," Mobola said over the comm. "The system is rebooting. It'll be about ten minutes before we have full use of the hyperdrive."

"Use that time to come back to the bridge," Neela said. "And hurry."

Salt and Pepper glanced at each other, the momentary expressions of relief having vanished from their faces.

"Captain, what the hell's going on?" Salt said.

Another thing I'll need to explain on the way," Xerx said. "But hopefully, it won't be as bad as this."

"You ... hope?" Pepper said.

"It's all I can do," Xerx said, leading the way back through the corridor away from the engine chamber, "considering my track record for luck today."

TEN

S hadow Star: Dorado System: 21 Light-Years from
Rickman's Pulsar

"Why do I keep on running into you naked?" Kairen asked.

He had long accepted that with the crew always on the go, the
Shadow Star seemed a much smaller vessel than he'd originally
thought. It took somewhat longer, however, to accept the crew's
various eccentricities, especially those of Pip. Pip, the diminutive
woman that lay on the table before Kairen, reached to adjust the
edge of her compression suit that had been rolled down to her hips.
She moved slowly so as not to interrupt Ike's meticulous engraving
with the tattoo needle. The older man paused his painting to wave
Kairen's way, Pip's paper-white skin, indicative of the Imperium's
genetically-engineered "tanks," making the intricate line art from
a prior session more brilliant than the cornucopia of tribal tattoos
on his sinewy arm.

"I dunno," Pip said. "You're the one who walked in here. And as
you can see, I'm not naked."

"Naked enough," Kairen muttered.

Pip rolled her eyes. "Anyway... in answer to your question
before you left, if you used a TTSV filing system and linked it to
a HR7 manager account with the new PPS-D6R firmware update,
you'll be able to access records in a fraction of the time."

"And thus continues the nerd talk," Ike said, punctuating his quip with a soft chuckle.

"I'm already running HR8-PS with the new PPS-D4B 2.6.1," Kairen retorted. He ran his hand through the long fall of blonde hair on the unshaved portion of his head. "I'm telling you it's a hardware issue—" He blinked and then frowned, turning slightly away, a look of discomfort crossing his face. "Look, I'm sorry, but how the hell can you stand that?"

"So says the guy who works in sickbay spending his time patching up the crew?" Pip flashed Kairen a sideways grin.

"Being poked repeatedly with needles is a different thing," Kairen replied.

Pip raised her arms, both covered in depictions of a kind of multi-eyed fish resembling koi from a fancy pond.

"And you had a lot of ties with Yakuza, if I'm not mistaken," Pip said, raising an eyebrow. "You must've seen them do this before."

"Couldn't stand watching that either."

"Wuss."

"Not that I care, but I'm curious," Ike chimed in. "Just what were you two talking about before all this?"

"Medical equipment," the two said in unison, after which Pip continued. "He thinks that a—"

Her eyes suddenly went wide. "Wait a minute," she said, indicating for Ike to stop. He put away the tattooing needle and wiped away the excess ink with a linen cloth as Pip reached for the cranial jack above her ear. There was a lengthy, wordless pause before she suddenly slipped off the table. Kairen and Ike watched expectantly as Pip, no taller than a twelve-year-old, maneuvered her arms into the top part of her compression suit, heading toward the door at the room's opposite end.

"Hey, Captain, I'm getting a ping from the hyperspace beacon near grid 439 by 217," Pip announced, her fingers returning to her jack. There was another pause, followed by a roll of her eyes. "Yeah, the Pulsar region."

After a moment, she turned to face her crewmates. She made a wordless swirling motion with her fingers—a gesture both men were familiar with.

"Yeah, EDDIE's firing up the main drive now," she said over her comm, her gaze at last settling upon Ike as she set to work on the seals to her suit. "We bounce in five."

"Rickman's Pulsar?" Kairen asked, and Pip nodded. "Damn, a distress call from that hellhole?"

"Yep," Pip replied as she followed Ike toward the bridge. Kairen took the rear. "Hell just called and dared us to rescue a friend."

Xerx and his beleaguered Felyan crewmates arrived on the bridge, exhausted after rushing through the now normal-length corridors, driven by fear. As Xerx expected, neither Salt nor Pepper took the news well of their trading the frying pan for the fire, but with little that could be done about it, they set to the next task with grim determination. Still, it was as if the universe had taken pity on them in at least one regard, as they had seen neither hide nor hair of the blue-haired girl the entire trip back. And even though Salt still maintained that his MAG shots had ended her, Xerx was not so easily convinced. Still, he counted his blessings, seeing the relieved smiles that Pepper and Mobola exchanged between each other and the painful-looking bear hug that Var had subsequently given both father and son.

"We've got multiple contacts on an intercept course," Neela said, once she reluctantly pulled away from the very welcome kiss she'd delivered to him. "There's also the problem of the engines being offline. We fell out of hyperspace too close to the pulsar's gravity well."

"Oh, wonderful!" Xerx said with a brief second's worth of joyless laughter. "So now we have a selection of gruesome deaths ahead of us: irradiated by the accretion disk, crushed by gravity, or both." At his wife's grim nod, he shook his head, suppressing his urge to break something in order to relieve his already seething fury at the day's rotten luck. After a moment, taking hold of his composure as best he could, he brushed the back of his fingers against Neela's cheek.

"*Kidege*, if we get through this, we're both going to need to seriously blow off some steam," Xerx murmured into her ear.

"That we will," Neela said in an equally hushed yet dusky tone. The slight but promising grin she flashed his way imbued him with a renewed will to focus yet again on not dying.

"Var, give the boys a chance to breathe so Pepper and Mobola can put their heads together," Xerx said, speaking to the shaggy Hara'Kya Felyan. Var complied, immediately releasing the two slightly crushed An'Kya Felyans from his long-armed vice grip.

"We need to know how much longer we have before the engines come online," Xerx said. "Salt, open a channel to the incoming ships. Var, man the weapons." He cast a pleading glance at Mobola. "We do have weapons, right?"

Mobola nodded. "The shutdown didn't affect weapons," she said.

At least one thing's in our favor, he thought, facing Neela. "*Kipenzi*, make sure the entrances to the bridge are sealed, full boarding protocol. I want this place to be a fortress. We don't need any more unpleasant surprises from our guest."

The crew set to work, and Xerx ascended the steps to the dais where the surrounding holos came alive with the ever-disorienting array of external images, displaying the monstrous sight of the Rickman's Pulsar: a luminescent orb with twin geysers spouting from its poles, propelling incomprehensible amounts of radiation into the cosmos. An accretion disc from a nearby star that had long ago been drawn into the pulsar's gravity well swirled about it, forming a vortex, like luminescent water in a drain.

"Bridge is sealed," Neela said as Xerx gripped the edges of a nearby console to steady himself.

"Mobola. Pepper. One of you, please give me some good news," Xerx said, at first unable to tear his eyes away from the sight of what was becoming even more what he suspected would be the last thing he would see. At last, he managed to shift his gaze down towards the two technicians—Mobola seated at a console, her own *msaidizi* connected to its circuits, while Pepper stood beside her, speaking confidentially. "We got an ETA on the engines?"

"They'll be coming back online in about five minutes," Mobola announced. "I'm trying to bypass some of the safety protocols to speed up the process..."

"...but there are more redundancies in the systems than on any modern ship," Pepper said, finishing her thought. "Makes me wonder if First Imperium standards were overly concerned with safety or if they were just plain paranoid."

"Five minutes doesn't seem too bad," Xerx said, beginning to feel a little better.

"But we're picking up speed every second. At this rate, the pulsar's gravity well will start to buckle the superstructure in less than three minutes."

"Of course it will," Xerx grumbled, his spirits yet again considerably diminished.

"On a more positive note, the ships are coming into weapons range," Var said.

"What about communications?"

"Nothing yet," Salt answered. Then a moment later. "Wait. I've got something. Looks like they're hailing us."

"Visual?" Xerx asked.

Var shook his head. "Audio only."

Not like they'd actually show their faces, Xerx thought. Of course, they would have more to lose than he would in seeing them, since he was familiar with more than a few members of his cousin Iriid's inner circle. The pirate king had inherited many enemies after he supplanted Montrose, the former monarch, and his supporters were none too happy about the change in management. If these Raiders were anyone Iriid knew, he'd personally go after their heads. Or worse, he'd send his wife.

"Breaker 99, this is Black Slaughter Rolling on the Fists of Monty." The voice over the comm audio was deceptively casual, though the signal crackled with static. With the massive amount of interference from the pulsar's radiation, it was a testament to the skill of his crew that they could make the incoming message as intelligible as it was. "I suggest you power down those weapons, boys, and roll me out the red carpet 'fore I release the hounds. Copy?"

The voice held the smugness of a face that Xerx imagined was quite punchable. And Xerx hoped he'd be able to meet the owner of that face just so he could deliver that punch.

"How many of them are out there?" he asked.

"Three that I can tell," Neela replied.

"Hard to get a bead on them too," Var added. "Interference from the pulsar." Suddenly, his eyes widened as a shriek erupted from his console. "Captain, they fired weapons!"

Xerx opened his mouth to speak, but Var's next words rendered the need for words null and void. "Wait. Low power impact, no damage."

"A warning shot?" Xerx said, unbelieving. "At a *warship*?"

"Either they're crazy or stupid," Salt commented, scowling as he glanced over at the hulking Felyan's readouts.

"Weapons are ready?" Xerx asked.

"Ready to go," Pepper replied. "Targeting system's kinda dicey because of the interference; Mobola's doing all she can about that, but the closer we get..."

"So no stalling for time," Xerx said, partly to himself. "Guess we don't have a choice then. Var, get ready to return fire. Use the MAG cannon. I wanna make a statement, not a warning."

"Is that a good idea?" Neela said.

"Give a pack of dogs a big enough show of strength and they run off," Xerx said, drawing up the positions of the Raiders' ships. They were hard to see, as the interference was now beginning to affect the clarity of the surrounding holos, but three bright circles lit up across the screen surrounding the ship, each blinking on and off in random patterns but holding position, matching their speed as the *Reckless* moved on its inexorable crash course with certain death.

"Tick tock, tick tock, big bird," the Raider said. "Waiting on that hangar bay to say 'ahh.' Come back."

"Guess they don't want to take the plunge with us," Xerx said. "At least we know why they won't get closer." He then paused, taken with a suddenly confusing notion. "So does anyone know why they're being so arrogant?"

"My guess is that they think that we're dead in the water," was Neela's suggestion. "But then again, they *are* Raiders. Have you ever known them to be humble?"

"Good point," Xerx replied. "Well, let's feed them a slice of humility, shall we?" He pointed at Var. "As soon as you can get a clear shot, take out the one off the port bow. Weapons free."

"Aye, Captain." A grin spread about the Hara'Kya Felyan's furry, striped muzzle as he gleefully punched in the firing sequence. Xerx looked down through viewports in the floor of the dais and watched as the nose of the *Reckless* appeared below him. Several panels shifted and swung open like a gigantic mechanical flower. In the center, the twin rails of the MAG cannon extended forward, blue arcs of electricity flashing between them in ever-increasing intensity. In moments, a flash of light engulfed the corresponding red-ringed target as ordinance tore through the smaller craft like a sledgehammer on an empty eggshell. Xerx watched with satisfaction as masticated fragments of the destroyed craft drifted outward into space, and others followed the *Reckless* on its inexorable course.

"They're not leaving," Xerx said, watching as the other red-ringed ships sat motionless.

"Pretty obvious," Salt said.

"Not the time, dad," Pepper snapped.

"Mobola, were you able to shave any more time 'til the engines are back online?" Xerx asked, now beginning to feel a very distinct sense of unease.

"Not enough, captain," Mobola replied, her tone dismal.

A pit that could consume a star grew in Xerx's stomach as he came to the realization that he probably made a big mistake. If he surrendered, there might have been a chance that the Raiders could have somehow towed the *Reckless* away from the pulsar—though he had no idea how. But he'd just taken out one of their ships while they were still stuck in this gravitational mire. God only knew what they'd do now.

He did not have long to wait, as at that moment, the Raider's voice crackled across the comm. His tone was now much harder and crueler.

"You know, I was going to drag your girl out of the hell's mouth and just sell you to Zade, so you could at least have a fighting chance in their mines. But now, I think I'll just blow her into salvageable parts and sift through what's left. Come back."

"Incoming projectiles," Var announced on the tail of the broadcast. "Interference is making the number hard to count."

"Launch countermeasures," Xerx said. "Once that's done, light 'em up. I want them to pay for every scrap they get off this ship with their collective asses. I want them to regret ever deciding to take on the *Reckless*."

Mobola spoke up. "That might not be wise, Captain. If we start launching more projectiles, the reaction to the force that we expel will launch us in the opposite direction, speeding us up."

"It's either that or get chunks blown out of my ship," Xerx replied, venting his frustration with a loud huff that made Mobola jump. "Do it, Var," he said to the Felyan, hating the command he'd just given.

Var growled—this time a sound of frustration rather than anticipation.

"What's wrong?" Xerx asked, watching the hazy holos as multiple green circles fanned out toward the orange circles that represented fire from the Raiders' weapons. Space lit up with multiple subsequent flashes as the circles connected.

"Countermeasures were deployed, but..." Visibly frustrated, he typed at his console, his growl deepening. "The ship shut me out of weapons."

"Mobola, you know anything about this?"

"Ah, the ship has ... switched over to shields," Mobola replied, nearly tripping over her words.

"Please don't tell me you did this," Xerx asked, about to rip apart the nearest console if this turned out to be yet another stroke of his bad luck.

"No, it was a reactive subroutine," she replied.

"It's like the ship knew the danger of what you were trying to do and offered a different strategy," Neela commented.

"Rather, the ship is protecting itself from the increased gravity," Pepper added, reading the graphs that appeared on Mobola's screen. "It will protect us from the Raiders' weapons as well, so there's something to be thankful for."

"Nevertheless, I think we need to learn more about this ship when we're not busy trying not to die," Neela said.

"So the ship bought us some time," Xerx mused, feeling somewhat better.

"Not much, but some," Neela said.

Mobola yelped. The noise she made was so loud and sudden that it caused everyone on the bridge to jump. But the noise that she made, this time, was not a frightened one. Still, it did not prevent Xerx from cursing louder than he'd had the whole day.

"Well, you mind telling us what you nearly scared the crap out of us for?" Xerx asked the young technician, both annoyed and at the same time regaining his composure.

"The power drain when weapons went offline," Mobola said, for once not fazed by his reaction. "It was what we needed." She turned toward the dais with the brightest grin that Xerx thought he had ever seen from her. "We have grav drives again!"

ELEVEN

"So what are we waiting for, an invitation?" Salt exclaimed, making frantic gestures toward the surrounding holos. "Let's get the hell outta here!"

Xerx had been about to give the order, but Mobola spoke first. "It's not that easy."

Xerx, suddenly feeling like a deflated balloon, gave a blank stare. "Wait. Didn't you just say that we have our grav drives back?"

"Yes, but we don't have full thrust," Mobola explained. "The power drain on the tesseract is too much with the shields at maximum. We won't fall into the pulsar, but we're still dead in the water."

"What do we have to do then, get out and push?" Xerx asked, irritation making a very unwelcome return to his nerves.

Pepper looked away from his console with a look of frustration to which Xerx could very much relate right now. "If we didn't have to fight gravity *and* Raiders at the same time, we'd be able to divert more power from the shields to the drives."

Xerx felt a slight vibration rumble through his feet. Instantly, the console beside Var made a flat buzzing noise.

"They're firing on us, aren't they?" Xerx said.

"Yes," Var answered. "Multiple contacts, mid-terawatt MAG cannons. Shields should hold their own though."

"Well, that's a relief," Xerx commented.

"But it'll slow down any recharge," Salt said.

"And draw more power from the tesseract." Var's muzzle wrinkled into a snarl. "Any fluctuations in the power feed and—"

"Right," Xerx said in a monotone voice. "Weapons back online?"

"That's a negative," Var replied. "But if what the small lady says is correct, we probably don't want them online right now anyway."

"I'm open to suggestions, guys," Xerx said. It was a comment to which the crew responded with awkward, disheartening silence.

Xerx sank to his knees at the edge of the dais, resting his head on the front end of a console, more discouraged than he'd ever felt. He was the unofficial leader of this bunch, but at the moment, he never felt more helpless. The *Reckless*, the last of the warships of the centuries-dead First Imperium, was bequeathed to him by his father on what he felt was the happiest day of his life since his marriage to Neela. But right now, the amount of trouble this ship had brought in the span of a day made him wonder if it was somehow cursed. Between the intruder that they had picked up from Siberna, the constant system issues, and the very real threat of either a swift death in a pulsar or capture by Raiders and a subsequent life of degradation at the hands of Zadian slavers, he supposed he might have been better off autopiloting it into the nearest star.

A rock and a fucking hard place.

"I am going to have such a headache if we get out of this," he whispered, as the rumblings of continued weapons' fire shook the framework of the ship beneath his feet. For a moment, his mind touched on the memory of Neela's implied assurance for later. *And it's probably one that even sex won't cure. I'm sorry,* kidege.

"Ah, Captain, I'm picking up some weird music coming through," Salt announced, refocusing Xerx's attention. He noticed Neela, halfway up the ramp to the dais, pausing in her tracks.

"Did you say 'weird music'?" she asked before he could.

"Yeah. It's not coming from the Raiders' broadcasts either." The younger Felyan re-checked his readouts. "At least not as far as I can tell."

"*Kipenzi*, search for new contacts, or familiar IFFs," Xerx said to his wife, who turned and descended the ramp, rounding the dais to return to her console. "Salt, patch the music through, but turn down the volume before you do. If I know who it is, she likes to make an entrance in a big way."

A moment later, the comm reverberated with the driving notes of guitars and drums, played at a pulse-pounding speed amidst raucous lyrics.

"Is that what I think it its?" Var's long ears twitched with familiarity over the raucous din of melodies.

"Sounds like *Run to the Hills* to me," Xerx said, bemused at the old Iron Maiden tune. "Well, you know how they like to make an entrance."

"Contact confirmed." Neela turned toward her husband, her lips spread in a very wide, very much relieved, grin. "*Shadow Star* dropping out of hyperspace. Broadwave Audio broadcast coming in."

"Breaker 99, this is the Pocket Rocket rolling aboard the one and only *Shadow Star*." The voice was high-pitched, almost child-like—clearly Pip's. She thoroughly enjoyed her position as the ship's spokesperson, and she sent her messages with a very enthusiastic flourish. In return, the Raiders' comm signal erupted into a din of panicked chatter. "I got us a holler to the Big Dogs out there sniffing blood, come on?"

Static carried over the speakers with no discernible answer before Pip spoke again.

"Aww, boys, don't be like that. Well, for what it's worth, this is your first and only warning to disengage and jump back to your playpen. We're twenty seconds out from drop. If you're still there by then, your asses are ours. Come back?"

Moments later, the flash of a hyperspace corridor opened on the *Reckless'* starboard bow, spitting out the blunt arrowhead shape of the *Shadow Star*—yet another relic of the First Imperium as the *Reckless* had been. One Raider screamed for all hands to open fire, and space was lit up with lances of blue light that arced toward the huge transport ship. Explosions bloomed across its surface, but the vessel flew on, blue flashes lancing over the hull as its shields absorbed the impacts. It made a full stop directly ahead of the *Reckless*, holding the two Raider vessels between them.

"Breaker 4-5, now you're hearing from the captain, Android Eater," a different, more mature voice announced over the comm, her casual words spoken with a distinct threatening edge. "You were warned to disengage and leave. You have one last chance to turn tail and bounce before I unleash my own dogs. Come back?"

"We've got a visual coming from the *Shadow Star*," Salt said.

"Let's see it," Xerx replied.

A new holo overlapped the holos of surrounding space: a view of the crew of the *Shadow Star*, with the image of Paige—the source of the voice—dominating. The captain's purple hair was flipped over her artificial eye but not enough to hide the surrounding scars created by the androids that had nearly tore her apart. Her black and silver bionic arms were crossed as a crooked smile played at the edge of her mouth, which was dressed with black lipstick. Behind, her crew sat at their respective consoles. Ike, Brogan, and Kairen were the only three males; the first two were burly and screamed "mercenary." The former was darker-skinned and tattooed heavily, while the latter sported even more cybernetic parts than Paige. Kairen was just the opposite: slender, almost fully human, and obviously a thinker rather than a fighter, with a holographic HUD set in front of his left eye. The other three, Maria, Miranda, and Pip—arranged in order of size—held the monochrome skin and hair of Imperial tanks. The former was massive; the middle, average; and the latter, almost childishly petite.

"Thought you'd like a ringside seat for this," Paige said, giving a casual salute. She then looked down at Miranda, who sat at the starboard helm console between her two "sisters." "Cycle the MAG cannons, Miz. Open fire on the smaller one when ready."

On the background holos, Xerx and crew watched as four hatches slid open on the *Shadow Star's* sloped upper hull, from which the cannons' giant barrels extended. On the forward holo, Paige pressed a button on her console.

"Breaker 4-5, I gave you a chance. What comes next is on you. Come back?"

When the Raiders gave no response, Paige nodded at Miranda and snapped her fingers. The tank's console then lit up with targeting imagery and symbols of ordinance fire. Outside, the canons flashed blue with sparks of lighting as their deadly payload slammed into one of the smaller vessels. Pieces broke off the ship as shells tore through the hull as if it were paper, the pulsar's gravity doing the rest as its remains began to break apart. In seconds, a bilious tirade thundered across the comm at a very smug-looking Paige.

"Breaker 4-5, my ass! Now you can watch as I split that ship like a Rhoman ostrich egg! Come on!"

"I gave you a chance, but you threw it away." Paige's response was cold and razor-like as she abandoned the comm jargon. She nodded once more at Miranda, who again punched in the firing sequence. "Now I'll give you a TIP."

White streaks followed as a barrage of TIP missiles sped toward the helpless Raider ship. Flares lit up the night as missile after missile struck home, lightning flaring over its hull. Its power grid damaged, it drifted past the *Shadow Star*, now completely caught in the grip of the pulsar, firing missiles that sailed past the hulking ship as it impacted the *Reckless'* shields to no effect, their recoil merely pushing the Raiders farther toward the pulsar that awaited like a luminous geyser of death.

Gritting her teeth, Paige spoke to the doomed crew of the ship one last time.

"Don't fuck with my friends."

ELEVEN

On the underside of the *Shadow Star*, a series of hatches opened, and rotary launchers stacked with crippling Tactical Ion Pulse missiles descended from their alcoves. Its final missile barrage tore through its aft section. Maimed and hopelessly crippled, the vessel tumbled away toward its inevitable fate.

Amidst ecstatic cheers that erupted below the dais, Xerx staggered back and collapsed into the captain's seat at the platform's center, relief at last coursing through his beleaguered nerves. He blindly searched for his comm switch, then spoke in a rasping croak that physically reflected his mental exhaustion.

"Thanks, Paige. We owe you big time."

"Yes, you do," Paige replied dryly. "You're lucky we took on this contract. We'd been tracking Raider activity in this region as a favor to the pirate queen. Can you imagine if those amateurs at Dark Lights had gotten it? What a shit show that would've turned out to be."

Xerx could only laugh at the truth of her statement.

"I must admit, though, that compared to what I usually hear about you, this is deeper shit than what you normally find yourself in." Paige furrowed her brow. "And frankly, love, you look half-dead."

"I feel that way too," Xerx said. "And I think I can vouch for my crew when I say we all do. I've got a helluva story to tell you over a pint."

Paige grinned. "Really, now? Then come on over and tell it."

"Yeah, about that," Xerx drawled. "We still have one little problem to take care of. And your being here is better luck than we've been having all day."

"I gather this requires another favor of me?" Paige asked.

Xerx gave a slight grin. "Indeed it does."

TWELVE

Salt and Pepper stood close beside Xerx, this time armed with MAG rifles. Salt had protested at first, maintaining that their guest was probably dead ... until Neela had received a brief bio sign pinging near deck 2. Afterward, Xerx was certain that the older Felyan was thankful for the higher caliber weapon's added security. Having raided the emergency medical kits, he managed to patch up the wounds that he and his crewmates had taken and administered a generous dose of synthorphin that came down on their respective aches like the hammer of God. With his own MAG pistols reloaded, he waited at the airlock with Neela, pistol holstered at her side as well, to greet their guests.

"You really got yourself deep into shit this time," Paige said as she and her crew stepped off the airlock umbilical. Brogan, Ike, Maria, and Miranda were armed like a platoon about to drop into active combat. Miranda held a vicious-looking MAG rifle across her back; Maria gripped a massive ion cannon while Brogan and Ike ducked inside with ammo vests and shotguns. Only Pip stood unarmed beside her much taller tank sisters. Beside the company stood Artemis, whom he hadn't seen in the visual on the bridge. Petite, but taller than Pip, she was the spitting image of the woman that had been the bane of his crew's existence mere minutes ago, though with hot pink pigtails rather than long blue tresses, both held aloft by skull clasps. She wore a shirt that was as monochrome as the skin and hair of the tank trio, with one sleeve striped and the other bare, all above black leather pants and heavy-looking boots with silver buckles that ran all the way up the front. Instead of any kind of gun, a pair of knives were sheathed at her hips. Her rounded face sported multiple piercings in her eyebrows, the bridge of her nose, and lower lip, all set above a leather choker from which dangled a platinum female symbol.

"Wow," Xerx said in a flat tone, casting a cursory gaze over the weapon loadouts of Paige's crew. "Sure you couldn't find anything lower caliber?" He chuckled softly, but Neela smacked him smartly across his shoulder.

"Be nice, *kipenzi*," she said, making a gentle scowl. "They're doing us a favor."

"There's nothing here that will pierce the hull, dear," Paige assured him. "No need to worry."

"I'll take your word for it," Xerx said, keeping a wary eye on Maria's heavy-duty weapon. The massive tank smiled, broad and genuine, and even sweet, while Miranda seemed to look right through him, as if she were counting the air molecules behind his back.

Paige nodded toward Pip, who came to Neela's side. "Apparently you have a tech genius with you," she said. "Is that right?"

"Something like that," Neela replied. "Mobola is waiting for us on the bridge with Var." She then reached out her hand for Xerx's. Smiling, Xerx brought her closer and touched her forehead to his.

"Be safe, my love," his wife said.

"I'd say the odds are more in our favor now," Xerx replied, feeling a swell of renewed confidence. He gestured, indicating Paige and her crew before sharing one brief kiss. With amusement, he noticed the diminutive tank beside his wife rolling her eyes at the display of affection before following her back in the direction of the bridge. Letting out a sigh once she was out of earshot, he faced Salt and Pepper. "Last chance, guys. You don't have to do this with me. You can go with them."

"We have a bone to pick with this bitch too, you know," Salt reminded him, pointing to the bandage that rested prominently on the side of his head. "And there's no way in hell we'd let you go in alone."

"And for once, I think dad and I can agree," Pepper added. "We both want to put a round in her ass for what she put us through."

"I guess stubbornness can be a virtue," Xerx muttered, shaking his head. "Well, who wants to live forever? At least the ship won't be like a maze this time."

"You're unfamiliar with the layout of your own ship?" Paige asked, eyeing Xerx strangely.

"What? No!" Xerx protested. "Look, it's kind of a long story." He checked the holo from the bracelet that he still wore on his wrist. The signal had not changed: a closet in deck 2. He should have been comforted by this, but it only seemed to feed his edge of suspicion. "At least we know where to find her now... I think. She's got some kind of cloaking effect that kept us from getting a bead on her before you arrived, but if these devices are correct, she hasn't moved in over an hour. Still could be a trap though."

"That won't be a problem," Paige said, gesturing toward Artemis, standing close beside Maria, who in turn, spoke softly to her.

"Go find your sister," the big tank said.

"Sister?" Pepper's voice cracked a little.

"Long story," Paige replied with a wry grin as Artemis took the lead, drawing a knife and holding it at the ready as she skulked down the corridors. She made a fair bit of headway as Xerx and his crewmates, along with the *Shadow Star* crew followed along, forming a loose perimeter about them: Brogan and Maria taking point, and Miranda and Ike flanking. Paige moved alongside Xerx with Salt and Pepper following.

"So you mentioned the ship being like a maze," Paige said. "It seems we have time now for that story."

The group paused for a moment as it became clear that Artemis was nowhere to be seen.

"The fuck did she go?" Xerx said, a feeling of concern welling up in his gut. Then, to his relief, the bright pink of her hair emerged as she poked her head around the next corner ahead of them. She jerked her head and beckoned them to follow.

As Artemis led them along through the corridors and toward a nearby elevator, Xerx and his crewmates recounted the story of the hell that they had just gone through. Even now, with the memory of his near-capture still fresh, Xerx felt mildly uncomfortable in the elevator car as it descended.

Arriving on deck 2, just as he concluded the tale to a somewhat bewildered Paige, they spotted blood on the floor.

"I wonder what Pip will have to say about the way your ship functions?" Paige mused as Artemis gestured toward the entrance to the main rec lounge. "She loves a good mystery."

"I thought I did as well," Xerx said, "but after today, I'm not so sure." He indicated the droplets of blood that created a path leading to the rec room. "And at least I'm pretty certain this particular problem isn't working for the Doctor."

"You're still on about that?" Paige said, stifling a laugh. "I thought your cousin would've given up on that obsession of his. Don't tell me you're getting paranoid in your 'old age.'"

"Hey, I'm just doing Izz a favor," Xerx protested. "Besides, you ever known him to give up on someone who pissed him off?"

Paige hummed. "Touché. Still, it's been years."

A minute of concentrating silence passed as the team followed the blood trail and the pink-haired girl down the corridor toward the rec room.

"At least we're on the right track," Xerx said.

"Or she's throwing us off the trail," Salt said with somewhat less enthusiasm. "All I can smell is the blood. Good way to mask her true scent."

"Unlikely," Artemis said from her place ahead, not turning to face them. She touched the controls to the rec room doors, and they slid apart. The lounge was on the other side: a central hub to the gym, theater, reception hall, and pool. Each door was separated by holos that showed the magnificent view of space beyond and the flashing energy geysers of the pulsar. Seats were in a circular formation at the center of the lounge with a well-stocked bar at the very end. As they passed by, Xerx immediately noticed one bottle of very expensive Felyan brandy conspicuously missing and a copious amount of blood on the shelf where it used to stand. He frowned. That bottle had been part of Var's private stock. The big guy was going to blow a gasket.

"She ought to be dead with how much blood we've seen," Xerx remarked, noticing the increasing size of the blood droplets, now more like small puddles, transforming their trail into something like the beginnings of a murder scene.

"Not necessarily," Paige replied as Artemis paused by a closet next to the bar. She inclined her head toward the door, and the *Shadow Star* crew surrounded it, forming a semicircle and taking aim with their weapons. Paige stepped forward and stood beside Artemis, beckoning for Xerx and his crewmates to come forward.

Xerx swallowed, took aim with his pistols, and nodded to Paige. "Go ahead," Paige

said to Artemis, who pushed the door open.

What he saw was not at all what he expected.

She was huddled in the corner of the closet across from the broom and mop: the same girl that had beaten him down on Siberna, chased him into orbit, waylaid him and his crew on their way to engineering with traps, and had nearly killed them in an elevator, making half this day a living hell. Her long blue hair was unkempt; her black uniform was torn at the left arm, which was covered in blood, but she had no visible wounds. Beside her, the brandy bottle lay in pieces, with blood-covered shards littering the equally blood-soaked floor.

"Damn," Xerx whispered.

"Do we have the right girl?" Salt said, coming to his side. "The hell happened to her?"

The girl turned toward them, her large, golden eyes staring with a haunted look, her cheeks drawn, and her skin pallid. Her face, despite its gauntness and lack of piercings, was nearly an exact replica of Artemis.

"You gave me a lot of trouble," Xerx said, finding his voice. Emotions wrestled within him at the pathetic creature that now sat in front of him, seemingly helpless, but prior experience kept him at a healthy distance as he debated internally over what to do. "You damn near killed me several times and cleaned the clocks of both my crewmates. If it weren't for you, we would've gotten out of this mess a hell of a lot quicker."

The girl just stared, as if she were an injured dog that had just been beaten by a remorseless master.

"You don't have anything to say for yourself at all?" Xerx said, feeling a particular and very familiar annoyance well up in the back of his mind. Frustration grew with every memory, from the beatdown he received in Pit Town, to barely escaping Siberna with his life, and finally, to each frustrating and painful delay in his trip to save them all from a crushing death in the bowels of a pulsar.

"Fine, then," he said tersely, raising his pistols to her head. This time he would be certain to not leave enough of a head to heal. "Be thankful that I'm not going to let you suffer like you did to us."

He gripped his pistols tighter. He set his finger on the trigger, placing pressure on it...

From his left, a hand covered with stripes gently pushed his arm down. Shifting his gaze, he saw Artemis shaking her head.

"No," she said, walking past Xerx and into the closet.

"Ah, okay," Paige replied, nonplussed. She and Xerx watched as Artemis walked past the assembly and into the closet, where she knelt down and embraced the emaciated girl.

"I thought you hated her," Paige said.

"It's true that I hold no love for my sister," Artemis answered. "However, she presents no threat to you at this time." She then fixed them with a chillingly serious look. "I won't let you harm her."

"Did we miss something?" Xerx asked. Utterly confused, he nevertheless holstered his guns as Paige ordered her crew to stand down, and he did the same with Salt and Pepper. Salt, having endured more from the girl than his son, showed a great deal more reluctance, but eventually he obeyed, casting an annoyed glance his way.

"We've had run-ins with this one," Paige said, watching as Artemis checked her bloody yet uninjured arm. "She calls herself Nemesis. There isn't much more than that, really. Those two are clones of someone else; that much we know for sure. And they carry nanite self-repair systems beyond anything we've encountered before. I don't even think the Felyan Empire has anything as sophisticated as what they're packing."

Pepper hissed in disgust, waving a hand at the blood and glass. "But why would she even do that to herself?"

"You defeated her," Artemis said, still checking over her strangely compliant twin. "Failure is not something the ISID tolerate to any great degree. She's frightened of what they might do."

Paige looked down at Artemis with a frown. "Would *he* do that to her?"

Artemis shook her head. "Not him."

"Who's *he*?" asked Xerx.

"Her boss," Paige said. "We don't know much about him, but we know that Nemesis adores him, and he treats her like a daughter. I don't think he'd hurt a hair on her head. But *his* bosses are another story."

"Well, she was downright brutal when she was keeping my crew on the ropes," Xerx mused aloud before returning his attention to Artemis. "I'm guessing it runs in the family?"

Salt grunted. "So what do we do with her?"

"If she's here, then she won't be alone," Maria said, speaking up for the first time. "Her handler should be skulking about nearby." She cast a sideways glance at Paige. "Don't you think, Captain?"

"Ah, Captain?" A voice crackled over the comm, breaking into the conversation. The way Paige smiled was indication enough that it was Kairen, who was holding down the proverbial fort aboard the *Shadow Star*.

"Yes, love?" Paige said.

"We have an incoming message."

"Origin?"

"I can't pinpoint it," Kairen replied. "I ran it by Pip. She says it's probably from a cloaked ship or something."

"Makes sense," Paige said. "Put it through."

"Coming in visual," Kairen said, and Paige gestured toward the middle of the company. A diode emitter opened up in her palm, and the translucent image of a man stood before them. Sunglasses concealed his eyes; he was wide-framed and immaculately dressed in a black business suit and green tie, but otherwise nondescript in a way that suggested that it was designed to be that way. Though Xerx had never seen the man before, Paige spoke to him with a great deal of familiarity.

"Four," she said with a cordial nod.

"Captain Wilson," the man—Four—said. "We meet again." He then glanced toward the closet. "I believe you have something that belongs to me."

Mobola could only stare, slack-jawed and horrified, and feeling just the slightest bit light-headed at the sight that greeted her eyes. This pint-sized near-stranger from the *Shadow Star* had practically waltzed onto the bridge with Neela, broadcasting ridiculous levels of confidence as she conducted what equaled to a hostile takeover of her console with the most boisterous of declarations.

"Okay, folks, amateur hour is over," she'd said. "The pros have come to save the day!" Mobola would have laughed had she not proceeded to do what she did next.

"What's the matter?" Pip's tone was casual in spite of what Mobola was seeing. "You look like you're about to toss your cookies all over your console."

"What's the *matter?*" Mobola only stared, gesticulating, her eyes frozen and wide on the tiny tank—more specifically, her left arm, into which she was shoving a data spike, connected to an adaptor fitted into the console in front of her. "How can you... I mean, doesn't that hurt?"

"Oh, right," Pip said, pausing as the connection was made with a small *click*. At least there wasn't any blood; Mobola didn't know if she would be able to endure that. "I forgot how newbies take to this kind of thing." The tiny woman then reached out and patted her on the stomach. "Just keep those cookies in there nice and tight, 'kay? And, well, to answer your question, you get used to it after a while. I'm a tech tank, after all. Used to be connected to computers constantly. Long story. But all you need to know is that I can swim through computer systems like a fish in water. Never met a memory archives I couldn't find my way around."

Mobola swallowed, hoping the taste at the back of her throat wasn't bile, still unable to stop staring at what was essentially this petite, monochrome woman maiming herself. She nodded absently before Pip snapped her fingers in front of her eyes. She jumped in surprise; then, she blinked, breaking her half-horrified, half-fascinated trance.

"Hey, wake up. We gonna do this thing, or what?"

"Ah, yes," Mobola shook her head to clear her mind and hopefully shake off the burgeoning nausea. "But so you know, the *Reckless* is not quite like most ships."

"Been there, done that," Pip said with an air of unbridled confidence. "It's a First Imperium relic, like the *Shadow Star*, so I can't imagine how this could possibly be any different."

Mobola shrugged, helpless. "Then I guess I will defer to your advice," she said, cringing inwardly at how pathetic she sounded.

"Don't worry." Pip grinned with laid-back ease as she climbed into the adjoining seat and reclined. "We'll have all the bugs shaken out before you know it!"

Mobola willed the connection to activate through her *msaidizi*, thankful that these were always connected to her body, and in a much less intrusive way. Feeling the connection activate, she closed her eyes as the digital signals transformed the darkness behind her eyelids into a white field.

Okay, kiddo...

Pip appeared before her, her avatar resembling a gleaming silver paladin from the ancient history of Old Earth, or rather, the fantasy role-playing virtual games that were popular on the more affluent worlds. It would have been impressive, had the design not matched her actual body proportions. Even in cyberspace, she seemed to be tiny.

Let's see if we can't optimize this son of a—*Wait. Is that all?*

What do you mean? Mobola said. *Is what all?* With this gleaming avatar now staring up at her, in a place where she usually was far more comfortable than in the real world, she felt an acute pang of self-consciousness. Cyberspace was her playground, where she could both be herself and yet nearly lose herself. And this diminutive tank was making her feel more awkward than she normally felt in her own skin.

Your avatar, Pip said, clarifying. She gestured toward her. *You're ... just you.*

Should I be more? Mobola asked. If mental projection simulacra were capable of blushing, she supposed she would have been turning a shade of red deep enough to be seen through her dark skin.

Pip laughed. *Oh, honey, you need a bigger imagination.*

But you're still the same size that you are in reality, Mobola said.

Yeah, and I've never been able to figure out why, Pip replied, shifting her stance out of obvious discomfort. *Others can be any size they want; I'm still just tiny old me. Size here ain't supposed to mean shit. But still, you can be anyone, so that's a plus. And that's why I like it here.* She then sighed. *But that's neither here nor there, I guess. So let's get to... um... wow.*

Pip's avatar paused, staring at the surrounding lattices of data and neon geometric tetrahedrons and dodecahedrons of nodes and command kernels. These hung from their respective system archives like bunches of grapes and shimmering vines that branched in fractal repetitions of right angles: a Euclidean vineyard that seemed to stretch into an infinity of visible white noise.

Is something wrong? Mobola asked.

Ah... um... Pip's pauldron arms hung by her side, like a person utterly dumbstruck with helplessness. *I have never seen this configuration before.*

It wasn't very intuitive for me either the first time I logged in, Mobola admitted.

Yeah... this must've been a custom job, Pip said. *I've seen a fuck-ton of systems, and I've never seen anything like this.*

Mobola, having extended system co-administrator privileges with Pip, shifted and materialized along with her as she zeroed in on a series of rotating strings of code that appeared and vanished about a singular node in rapid sequence.

Like this, the diminutive tank said, pausing the code's rapid-fire readouts for her to look over. *This looks like security code, but usually, something like that is kept in the middle of the archives unless it's brought to the forefront for analysis, or someone's cycling through codes, or something...*

Wait. Mobola brought the strings of code to her and expanded its readouts. She willed her bionics to run an analysis, which manifested itself as a series of green rectangles that encapsulated the scrolling data at the same rate as it appeared. *Did you say 'cycling through codes'?*

Yeah, kind of like you just—holy shit! How fast are you running that program?

Mobola paused, the rectangles freezing in the middle of their subsuming of the scrolling code. *I'm not running any program.*

You mean you're doing all that by yourself?

It's my biotech, Mobola said. *It was state-of-the-art on Mandela I when I had it installed.*

Pip gave a low whistle. *Whoa. I didn't think they made stuff like that. I mean, it's light-years behind my own implants but still impressive.*

This is commonplace back home, Mobola said, inwardly cringing as her tone turned involuntarily wistful at the mention of her lost homeworld.

Now I know why the Imperium took it over, Pip said, her voice softening. *I'm sorry.*

Without another word, Mobola forced her concentration away from that still open wound and completed her analysis... then nearly shattered the code by the sheer force of her pushing it away. The representational limbs of her avatar curled in horror as a wave of light caused the system archives to shudder, a digital jangling noise echoing into the distanceless void.

What's wrong? Pip said.

That code isn't internal to the ship, Mobola replied, her voice tense with fright. *It's an algorithm, cycling through a combination lock, but it's bypassing the main security subroutines.*

Mobola watched as Pip ran her scanning programs through the code lines, lattices of data overlapping the cascade of code before them: blue on yellow, combining into a neon green.

Damn, she said after a moment more. *You're right. You're being hacked.*

A bolt of electric terror ran through Mobola as she pinpointed the location of the code breach and then activated her comm. She had been about to warn the captain when a shimmer of code abruptly slammed unbidden through the geometric patterns of the system and even through the code lines that she and Pip had analyzed. As if everything had been suddenly dipped in blood, the system color scheme changed from a kaleidoscope of hues amidst infinite white, to a uniform deep red. A laser light show of electric blue formed a web of new code lines throughout the system, and relaying to each monitor's archives and nodes, conveying the same message.

INTRUDER ALERT.

Well, well, well, Pip said, placing her arms at her hips. *I think I know who did the custom job on this system now.*

Who? Mobola sked.

It did it on its own.

"Something that belongs to you?" Paige said with a shrewd grin. "I don't see your name on her ass."

Four's face showed not a ripple of amusement as he appeared to ignore Paige and instead set his attention on Xerx. "Captain Paraska, I'm sure my protégé has given you a difficult time, but it appears you're none the worse for wear for it." He stole a glance back toward Nemesis, whom Artemis now held cradled in her arms. "She, on the other hand, is clearly in need of ... assistance. And so, to make this situation easy on the both of us, all I ask is that you relinquish her to me. In exchange, we will make no more attempts to acquire you."

"So this was all about you wanting to kidnap me." Xerx phrased it as a statement, though he was both relieved that it never was whom he'd originally suspected was behind this. As things now stood, he was more irritated than surprised to learn that this black-suited stranger had been behind this unbelievably long day. "And I suppose that your reasons are need-to-know?"

The corner of Four's mouth twitched, as if he were stifling a grin.

"As far as needing to know is concerned, you only 'need to know' that my superiors had plans for you. But this mission became a washout due to unforeseen circumstances. And I doubt anyone on my end will want to try this tactic a second time, knowing you're being watched by allies of the pirate clans." He then folded his hands as he appeared to sit down on an invisible chair. "So all that is needed is to retrieve Nemesis, and she and I will never again darken your proverbial doorstep."

"I could turn her over to the Alliance," Xerx said, testing the waters.

"That would be ... inadvisable," Four replied. "The Alliance doesn't have the resources to deal with her kind, I'm afraid. And I assure you, she would end up being far more trouble than she was worth."

Not one flicker had come to his facial features, but Xerx could feel the veiled threat in the man's words, enough to where he decided to forego that plan. The rest of the conversation, however, had sounded very casual and businesslike—almost friendly. The man was a smooth operator, no doubt, but as for whether or not he could be trusted, was a different matter entirely.

But what else could he do?

"I think it's best that we give her back," Paige suggested. "I've had more experience with her than you, and I can say that she has been just as much a help as a hindrance."

"That's of little comfort," Xerx said.

"Wasn't supposed to be, Chicken," Paige replied. "I'm just being honest." She inclined her head toward the closet. "That's the nature of this particular beast: might save your life; might steal your ship."

Xerx scowled. Something told him that in giving this girl away, he was blowing some kind of golden opportunity, but what mattered was the moment. And at this moment, his needs and the needs of his ship and crew were obvious. In every way, they trumped the need to keep a prisoner.

"You can take her," he said to Four. "I've half a mind to stuff her into a spacesuit and kick her out the nearest airlock for you to pick her up, but I'll be nice. Where do you want to meet?"

"We can meet on Siberna," Four replied. "I'll arrange the meeting place as soon as I arrive."

"Why not pick her up now?" Xerx said.

"My good Captain." Four's voice was now openly condescending. "There's a time and place for everything. Besides, I believe you'll need some time to fix the matter on your ship. It's far from resolved, after all."

"What's that supposed to mean?"

"I guess I can give you this information as a gesture of good faith," Four said, "but I'm sure you would have figured it out on your own." Xerx then saw an actual smile play at the edge of the man's thin mouth. "You've been boarded."

"Bullshit" was what Xerx was about to say when the alarm klaxons drowned out his voice.

THIRTEEN

"**O**f course, the alarms would sound," Xerx said, the din of the alarm klaxons drowning out his cynical monotone. Honestly, if today had a pair of balls, he would have punched them with glee.

"Looks like your bad luck has dragged us in with you," he heard Paige comment.

"And so it seems that you have problems of your own once again," Four said. "I'll contact you when you finish dealing with it."

"So, helping people's not part of your talents?" Xerx asked.

"Well, I did let you know about the problem."

"Yeah, two seconds in advance!" Xerx replied, feeling a burning exasperation with the man's glib replies.

"Well, Captain Paraska, you don't have to thank me so profusely," Four answered. He flashed another wan smile as his image began to vanish. "I'll meet you in Siberna. For the time being, please look after my charge."

Fighting against the urge to uselessly swing at the fading hologram from Paige's emitter, Xerx brought up his wife on the comm. "What the hell happened?" he asked rhetorically.

"Intruder." Both his wife and Mobola had spoken, nearly in unison, only with Mobola adding "Captain," to her response.

"Location?"

"Near the deck 4 hardpoints," Mobola said. "They faked an authorized entry in one of the port side personnel docks."

"Sensors read fifteen in all," Neela warned. "They're nearing a junction in the corridors; it looks like they're splitting up."

"And they're moving fast," Mobola added.

"Then so are we," Xerx said. "Initiate emergency lockdown on the bridge."

"Way ahead of you, *kipenzi*," Neela replied.

Xerx turned his attention to Artemis, who still sat, or rather squatted, beside a near-comatose Nemesis. "Will she be safe here?"

"Hard to say," Artemis said. "She needs fuel. I'll stay with her."

"Good," Xerx replied, not quite certain of what she meant but confident that their first guest would be out of commission for the time being. Besides, if it was food the girl needed, the rec room had food in the refrigerator although it was only chips and pretzels.

"We're gonna need to go back the way we came and take care of some more unwanted company," Xerx said, grinning at Paige's crewmates. "Looks like you didn't bring those fancy guns for nothing after all."

"As long as they don't hit as hard as that weird-ass girl," Pepper said.

"I've dealt with Raiders back in my trader days," Salt commented with a nod. "At least you know what you're getting with them."

"*Kidege*, have Mobola bring up the Raiders' positions on our bracelets," Xerx said to his wife over the comm, "along with ours."

"She's patching now," Neela replied. After a moment, a series of green and red dots appeared on the map readout. "Pip says she's transferring the data to Paige's bionics."

"Got it, honey," Xerx heard Paige say, her finger to her temple and a faraway look as she gave a curt nod. Her gaze then focused back on him.

"They'll try to head for the bridge," she said, coming to his side.

Xerx shook his head. "They won't be able to get in."

"*They* don't know that." A sly grin spread across her dark lips. "And that means we can have fun with them at our leisure."

Xerx snorted. "I could use a little fun after today."

"Shall we, then?"

"Nothing to lose." Xerx returned Paige's smile, his tone a great deal more enthusiastic than before. With the help of Paige and her crew, this problem, he believed, would turn out to be little else than some much-needed stress relief.

Brogan tossed Paige a MAG pistol, which she primed. "I'm sure Pip is already working with Mobola to shut the corridor bulkheads to corral the Raiders and box them in," she said as the weapon made a satisfactory *click*. "She's good like that."

"Glad my talents are appreciated," the diminutive tank replied brightly over the comm. "And of course, I'm doing that. They'll be stuck on the deck near the elevator. Easy pickings."

"Also be a dear and shut that damn noise off," Paige said.

"Oops! Ah, sorry." The sheepish reply came from Mobola as the klaxons abruptly ceased, bringing a welcome, yet disconcerting silence. Paige and Xerx rounded up their respective crews and signaled for them to move out.

"Xerx, dear, we'll take the lead from here," Paige announced once everyone was packed inside the elevator. "We've been picking on these fuckers for months, so it'll be nice to have a little face-to-face with them."

In truth, and in spite of how grateful he was for the help, Xerx did happen to feel a vague tinge of irrational annoyance. After all, Paige was not supplanting his authority; she merely had the greater experience in this case. He quickly stifled his emotions as he allowed her men to take point.

"Yours would be better with flanking positions beside Brogan and Ike," Paige said. "There won't be any hard cover once we engage, so we'll have to rely on flash and smoke grenades to disorient them.

Raiders fight just as dirty, and they aren't known for being cautious. Expect a kamikaze run."

"Or two," Maria added.

"They *do* that?" Pepper half-whispered.

Paige frowned. "They're crazy and desperate," she said flatly. "Expect anything."

The door opened on deck 4, and Paige's component of the group fanned out from their position, while Xerx kept the rear. His eyes flitted back to the holo display from his bracelet as their guide.

"I think they heard us coming," he said as the bulkhead leading back toward the elevator shut behind them with a loud hiss, followed by the *clack* of a pressurized lock. "They're splitting up in different directions, trying to find other elevators."

"They probably don't know they're trapped yet," Pepper remarked. "They're gonna be pissed."

The display showed the Raiders approaching around the next T-junction. On Xerx's command, they slowed down. Maria and Miranda settled into a crouching position, weapons ready. Xerx checked the display. Three red dots, about ten meters away, rounded the corner that led to the junction. Paige scooted back until she knelt beside Xerx, pistol in one hand, sword in the other.

Maria turned around, her finger silently at her lips.

There came the tapping sound of an object bouncing through the corridor. Beyond the T-junction, it rolled on its approach. The whine of charging energy crescendoed.

"Down!" Maria cried out. She dropped her cannon and pushed her tank sister aside as she wedged herself into the entrance to the T-junction, spinning around to where her back faced the opening and hunching over. Her hands snapped to the sides of her head. "Cover your ears!"

Xerx slammed down on his ears just in time. The last thing he saw before he felt the concussion wave in his guts was Ike tackling Salt to the ground. The older Felyan had still been standing.

The sound was near-deafening even with his ears protected, and the concussion nearly made him sick. Then the bedlam started. Shots from MAG rifles thundered into the corridor as he stooped lower to the ground, but he heard a scream as he unplugged his ears. He watched as Brogan and Ike reached around Maria, with Miranda falling to her stomach and shooting below her. Paige's crew seemed unhurt thus far; Paige pinned herself against the wall, returning fire down the intersecting corridors. Salt, however, was lying on his side, clutching his right ear. A pit opened wide in Xerx's stomach as he crawled over to his crewmate's side, along with Pepper, who had a look of horror plastered on his face. He saw rivulets of blood running from the older Felyan's fingers. Salt groaned, uttering a string of oddly creative Felyan curses.

"Shit, he's popped an eardrum," Ike said. He reached down and turned the older Felyan's head to the side where there was no blood. "Looks like you stopped your left ear just in time."

"Won't ... stop ringing!" Salt exclaimed through a rictus of pain. Poor bastard. He seemed to be getting the worst of things over and over.

"We'll have Var patch you up after this is over," Xerx promised before flinching just as a round nearly grazed the edge of his nose. For a moment, Xerx froze, processing how close he'd come to his own mortality before a sudden blind fury exploded within him. He crawled forward to Maria's side. Two bodies lay strewn across the second T-junction beyond, with only one Raider left. Xerx wedged himself against the wall and returned fire around the giant tank's side, and for once today, he had a stroke of good luck as the Raider attempted to dive toward the other side of the junction. Xerx's round nailed him in the forehead, mid-dive.

Maria gave a signal to stop. "Clear," she announced, then crawled out into the open between her sister's legs. Maria followed suit, grabbing her ion cannon from the floor and flipping the size-able weapon onto her back before turning around. The armored plate on the back of her bustier-like armor was peppered with multiple dents from the Raiders' MAG rounds. Her arms were protected by spidersilk mesh, which would stop even accelerated rounds, but he imagined beneath the fabric was a series of massive bruises.

While Xerx helped Salt to his feet, Brogan tossed Ike a roll of gauze from one of the pouches of his combat vest. He tore off a piece and instructed the wounded Felyan to shove it into his ear to staunch the bleeding. Xerx shook his head, wondering just how much his crewmate now regretted volunteering for this sortie.

"Your ear must be ringing worse than the time you stood too close to the stadium speakers," Xerx said.

"I've had worse," Salt snorted with false bravado, but Xerx only needed to see the way he winced to see the lie in his words.

"I dunno," Xerx said. "This shit we're going through is way above what I've been paying you for."

Salt heaved a sigh. "Ship work always is."

They followed the *Shadow Star* crew into the corridor, Pepper once again staying close beside his beleaguered father, whom Ike was supporting on his shoulder. He seemed to give his son a reassuring gesture, but Xerx could only imagine his fury. His weapon was drawn and at his side, and Xerx could hear his constant, near-inaudible growl as they turned down the left hallway, where a Raider came running out of nowhere, screaming at the top of his lungs and brandishing a makeshift tomahawk. He tossed the weapon, which missed the crew by a mile as they ducked in unison. Then, the lone Raider fell to Brogan's shotgun, administered at point-blank range. Stepping over the body of the dead Raider, the company continued. After Salt assured Ike that he could walk on his own, Ike rejoined Brogan, flanking the right as Paige fell to the center. The grizzled Felyan's son, however, remained resolutely by his father's side, furtively checking the holo on his wrist display as often as Xerx was.

"We're about to have more company," Pepper announced after Xerx gave the command to the bridge to seal off the prior junction. The bulkhead slammed shut loudly behind them as the younger Felyan looked up from his wrist display, eyes like gold dishes. "They're coming in from the—"

Maria, with surprising speed, reached around the left side of the next T-junction. Her hands out of sight, Xerx saw her arms shake, followed immediately by the very familiar, sickening noise of bone snapping beneath flesh. A Raider's body collapsed to the ground from behind the corner, his neck twisted at an unnatural angle.

"Thanks for that, sweetie," Maria said to Pepper over her shoulder, with the most disturbingly sweet smile that Xerx had seen.

"We've got a couple left down the adjoining corridor at this junction," Pepper said. "They don't seem to be moving, but it's not like they have any place to go."

Just before they crossed the next T-junction, Miranda suddenly tackled Maria to the ground, just as a horizontal hail of MAG ammo tore through the perpendicular hallway amidst the screeching whine of another, larger round. Two thunderous explosions followed from behind the sealed bulkhead, rocking the deck plates in the corridor. Ike and Brogan whirled around, just as the lights blinked off. The emergency lights remained, casting the room in a dim half-light.

"*Kidege*, what the hell just happened?" Xerx asked his wife over the comm.

"They took out a power distribution node," Neela replied. "Mobola and Pip are working on getting it back online."

"Bastards are sneakier than we thought," Xerx heard Pip mention in the background, sounding both impressed and frustrated at the same time.

"I can barely see a thing now." Xerx began to hack and cough as the air grew heavier and harsher with the choking smell of burned metal, plastic, and plastic explosive particulates.

"Don't worry," Brogan said. "I can. Reopen the bulkhead."

Xerx was hesitant but capitulated, sinking to his knees with his crewmates. The power outage seemed to have been very specific as the paneling slid upward, opening the way down the corridor, which was now concealed in darkness. Brogan's rifle went off, momentarily lighting the darkness as yet another Raider was slammed down the hallway from the shot.

A shower of sparks rained from the wound, and Brogan cursed. "Shit! He's a cyborg!" Just then, the hallway erupted into light from the flash of a rifle. Brogan snarled as a shower of fluid that didn't smell at all like blood showered the side of Xerx's face. Brogan fell back, groaning as he hit the floor, a small hole in the shoulder of his metallic arm.

"I'm okay," he said. "Systems stopped the bleed-out." He gestured down the hallway. "He's still there. Take him out!"

Xerx could barely see anything but fired anyway, stifling his inclination to shoot wildly, remembering the exact area where Brogan had aimed. He pulled the trigger more times than he cared to count, sending round after round into the darkness, until a sudden eruption of erratic rifle fire lit up the corridor again. In flashing segments, like a video set to slow motion, he watched as the Raider tumbled to the ground.

"I think I got him," he said, daring to stand. He moved into the corridor beyond with careful steps, keeping his gun aimed. Ten feet down, he smelled the scent of blood and ran into the motionless figure, now clearly dead, sparks still seeping from the wound in his bionic arm, which twitched with random nerve pulses.

"That's another," Brogan said as he returned to the company. He was now sitting upright and patching the wound. He winced as a set of tweezers from his index finger removed the round while tiny servos erupted from the wound, assisting with its removal. "Rerouting circuitry," he announced, and after a couple of seconds, flexed his fingers. Smiling with satisfaction, he stood up with a grin. "Good job, Captain."

"And Pepper didn't even have to point that one out," Xerx said with no small amount of amusement. He glanced at the younger Felyan, gesturing to the corridors behind them. "Anyone else down that way?"

Pepper checked the readout and shook his head, gesturing back to the corridors ahead. "Not here, but they've holed themselves around the next bend; it's probably all that's left of 'em."

"They're fortifying their position," Xerx said to Paige, feeling much better about not having to ferret out a hanger-on. "Looks like someone didn't think things through."

He instructed Neela bring down the barricade again just as he noticed Miranda dive across the T-junction, just missing a renewed barrage of ammo from whatever weapon had been placed at the end of the adjoining corridor. The mostly silent tank announced a frag grenade as Paige and company stepped back. Salt and Pepper followed suit as the weapon bounced down the corridor and detonated with another flash of light and panel-shaking vibrations. They waited for a moment, and Paige took a chance, reaching around Maria's Amazonian side and firing down the corridor. The whine of the weapon's barrels started yet again, and she jerked back as another hundred rounds transformed the path into a death trap.

Well, that's one way to stick a pin in my ego, Xerx thought as Paige groaned.

"A rotary MAG," the captain said. "Lovely fucking day this is."

"Yep, they're fortifying all right," Ike said. "That thing's gonna keep us busy for a hot minute."

"Xerxes Paraska!" someone had called from down that perpendicular corridor. "Yeah, I know this is your ship. Your reputation precedes you. Gonna be real nice having your head to send back to Rhoma, all gift-wrapped for your usurping cousin. What's the matter? Can't fight your own battles, so you get the Android Eater and her bitches to do your dirty work?"

"So says the man who scalps ships still in hyperspace?" Xerx taunted back. "You're gonna have to work for this head if you want it and fly it out of here—oh! That's right; you don't have a ship, do you?" He paused to let the full sting of his invective sink in. "But I'm pretty sure if you ask nicely, the pulsar might cough yours back up."

"You're dead, Paraska!" the Raider screamed back, followed by another round across the empty corridor. "You hear me? You're fucking dead! I'm gonna have myself two ships after we're done here. In fact, I'll probably just suit your bitch ass up and feed you to the pulsar!"

"Look who has a temper!" Xerx's voice with a derisive laugh—a laugh that was shortly drowned out by another round of ammo that tore across the empty hallway.

"The corridors past this junction double back around," Pepper said when the noise subsided yet again, and Xerx checked his holo. "Only eight more of those bastards."

Xerx checked his own readout. They were definitely holding position, protecting the red dots that lay at the far end of that adjoining corridor—whichever Raider it was who had brought that minigun aboard his ship. He turned toward Paige. "You have a plan?"

"Of a sort," Paige replied. "Miranda made it to the other side, so I think it's best if she handles the problem. I'll toss her my—"

She reached toward one of the swords sheathed at her back, her face frozen in an "oh" of surprise as she—and Xerx—noticed that the scabbard was now empty.

FOURTEEN

Xerx saw Paige's gaze shift away from him, as if she had noticed something coming from behind. He jumped at the subsequent tap on his shoulder and then nearly jumped out of his skin at the sight of Artemis.

"The fuck did you come from?" His exclamation caught the attention of his crew as well as Paige and her comrades. "And aren't you supposed to be looking after the other girl?"

The pink-haired girl pointed above, where Xerx noticed the opened grate of a ventilation duct. From the opening, a sudden scent of chlorine wafted through the air, distinct and strong, as if someone were doing some deep cleaning of a nearby restroom.

"Following," Artemis said and shifted her gaze past Xerx the combined crews, toward the hallway. Incidentally, neither Paige nor her crew seemed terribly surprised at the girl's sudden appearance.

"Wait, she's awake?" Xerx said, nonplussed. "But she was almost a damn vegetable."

"She needed fuel," Artemis replied.

Then it hit him. The scent of chorine... hadn't there been a bottle of cleaner beside her in that closet?

"She can drink bleach?" he asked Paige, who simply shrugged.

"Look at her go!" Ike exclaimed. Across the killzone that was the junction, Xerx saw a neon blue glow, cast by the frighteningly familiar tresses of Nemesis, again in full kick-ass mode, brandishing the captain's sword and running it through the neck of a Raider that leaped out from around the next corner. His scream broke into a wet, dying gurgle as she dropped him, then smoothly sheathed the weapon into the sternum of another Raider that had foolishly tried to sneak up on her.

Xerx gave a low whistle. "We didn't even see her coming."

"Is it really that surprising?" Paige answered with a playful grin. She made a cursory nod in Artemis' direction. "You've seen what she's capable of."

The rotary MAG finished emptying its next volley, and instantly, Miranda gave the signal to move before barreling forward. Everyone else followed, sliding like baseball players to home, across the killzone. Maria waited until everyone had passed before crossing herself. She paused just as the heavy weapon's familiar whine signified its readiness, only long enough to toss a grenade down the junction before it could dispense any more of the deadly payload. She then tumbled forward like a boulder to the safety of the other side, where everyone hunkered down with almost military precision. Xerx watched with dismay, expecting the detonation to not only destroy the weapon but also bring up yet another repair bill that would eat further into his tournament earnings.

"Don't panic, chicken," Paige whispered into his ear. "It's not that kind of grenade." She then lifted herself to a low squat. "Get ready, now; we're going to rush him."

Rather than another deafening explosion or flash, what sounded was more like a loud *pop*, as if someone had introduced a pin into a balloon ten times the size of a beach ball, which was followed by a dense, expanding smoke cloud that filled the junction. Maria bounced back to all fours and launched herself forward, making a hairpin turn down the adjoining hallway as Paige and her crew followed the massive tank. With a speed that suggested that her ion cannon weighed less than a loaf of bread, Maria flipped the weapon off of her back and into firing position, vanishing into the cloud. Xerx could only make out shadows, but there had certainly been someone operating the rotary MAG. The hall echoed with coughing, which Maria put a stop to, as she appeared to full-on head butt the Raider. There was a sound of two bodies impacting, followed by a choked "Oof!" which ended with a loud, metallic clatter. From out of the cloud, the unconscious body of the Raider slid, a massive knot on his tattooed forehead.

What Xerx had not expected was the subsequent priming of a weapon, followed by the piercing whine of Maria's ion canon. A subdued flash came from within the blinding miasma, followed by Maria's cheerful announcement.

"All clear," the massive tank had said before stepping out from the cloud, carrying the ponderous weapon on her shoulder as if it were a simple child's toy. The rear part of it was releasing its own black cloud that transformed into a gray smudge amidst now-thinning clouds.

"Got a new toy, I see?" Paige said.

"Rotary MAG got toasted," Maria answered, "but it can be salvaged." She made a grin that Xerx had only seen before on children that had won the grand prize at a carnival. "It's a MA-180 with a custom rig and variable ammo setup. Might be worth keeping."

"Indeed," Paige said with an approving nod. "Good work. Leave it here for now. We can fix it back on the ship."

"How the hell did they get something that big aboard this ship anyway?" Salt wondered aloud.

"I've been asking myself that question about the big tank," Pepper remarked under his breath—a quip to which Xerx had to suppress a chuckle.

"Ike. Brogan. Head that way." She gestured toward the corridor that Nemesis had gone down. "Miranda, take point. The rest come with me." She glanced at Pepper. "They loop and connect to each other, right?"

The younger Felyan glanced at his bracelet's holo and nodded.

"Good. We've got them right where we want them. Hopefully, Nemesis won't have hogged all the action. Shoot anything that moves."

The giant tank placed the damaged rotary MAG on the ground and threw her ion cannon over her shoulder with glee as Paige stood beside her with pistols aimed.

They met no opposition coming out of the nearly dissipated smoke as they rounded the corner. But Xerx could hear sounds of battle in the subdued light with more flashes of blue.

"Bitch better not break my sword," Paige remarked as she and Maria quickened her pace. At the first right angle, they both froze in their tracks as the distinctive thumping of MAG rounds arose amidst the growing din. Maria made a stern halting gesture before Xerx saw the shadow. She then gestured to Paige, who fired just as Xerx heard the hurried footsteps. The shot hit the Raider that had rounded the corner square in the chest. His corpse spun across the floor as Xerx saw more flashes of blue and heard the now nearby sounds of battle and quick death.

Maria skidded into the middle of the hallway, then braced herself into a rooted stance before cutting loose with her ion canon. Buoyed by her audacity, Xerx and Paige took hard cover against the wall and fired around the corner at the five Raiders that remained. They had fortified their position well, judging from the armored weapons cases strewn about the middle of the floor, but they hadn't counted on a blue-haired murder machine coming in from behind. While Ike, Brogan, and Maria took potshots at the remaining forces across the way, a very different battle was going on in the midst: a macabre fusion of death and disco.

Nemesis's glowing neon blue hair flared as it rippled behind her: a burning cold azure flame as she faced off against two Raiders, armed only with knives in that spinning dance of death, skilled just enough with their respective blades to temporarily hold their own against this assassin and the inevitable end she brought at terrifying speed. One, however, brandished a blade that appeared to be something more akin to a meat cleaver than any kind of a weapon. He was not hard to single out; he was the biggest that Xerx had seen among the lot, and interestingly enough, the hairiest, wearing a spotted coat of jackal ape hide, and sporting a braided beard of dirty red and silver. The unusual shape of the marks on his bare arms was a telltale sign of subdermal augmentation.

"I think we found the leader," Xerx said.

Xerx had been so fixated on the fight that he failed to notice the exact moment that Paige and Maria managed to pin down a pair of gun-wielding Raiders. Nemesis had decapitated the Raider opposite the red-haired one in the fight. But once Red locked eyes with Xerx, it was as if red was all he saw. And the smaller, blue-haired girl's luck took a very unexpected change for the worse.

"Paraska!" he bellowed, managing to casually slap Nemesis into the far wall, causing a human-sized dent. She slid down, Paige's borrowed sword hitting the floor with a resonant *clang* as she slumped over, unconscious. The Raider bounded over his other subordinates, ignoring Maria as she fired a shot that atomized the face of another one of the winnowing ranks beside him, and kicked the ion cannon to the side as he made a full-tilt, bull-like charge toward Xerx.

Xerx's arms automatically swept his MAG pistols into position. Not waiting to aim, he fired as quickly as his fingers would allow, one shot missing the man by nearly a foot from his right shoulder. The other sank square into the right bicep. Red roared in pain but closed the distance to Xerx, undaunted. Xerx forced down the rising wave of terror as he holstered the pistols and drew his knives. He readied himself to parry the blow as best as he could, but the sheer size of the man telegraphed the very painful experience he would certainly have of it.

An idea hit him nearly a second before it was too late. As Red's blade came down, ready to split him in two, he faked a parrying

stance—falling backward, letting all strength go out of his spine.
The blade missed, slashing mere inches away and cutting through
the air with a whistling hiss. Having put all of his weight into the
blow, the brute pitched forward uncontrollably. Like a spring that
had regained tension, Xerx bounced back upright and brought
the handle of his knife down on the back of the man's skull with
as much force as he could muster.

With a grunt, the man hit the floor with a resounding *thud* that
shook the deck. Xerx waited for a moment, realizing that outside
of the blood rushing through his temples, the deck had become
eerily silent. Sheathing his knives, he drew a single pistol and
approached Red cautiously. He kicked away the giant blade, now
bereft of a wielder, letting it slide across the floor behind him.

He tapped the Raider's shoulder with his boot. He was
breathing, but otherwise motionless. He smelled like a rusted dis-
tillery. Nice coat, though. It reminded him of the one his friend
Tyger often wore, even in Siberna's perpetual heat.

With a sudden vice-like grip at his ankle, the world flipped
upside down. All Xerx remembered of it was a roar and a multi-
tude of forces sending him into what felt like the loving embrace
of steel and fiberglass. Lightning bolts crackled behind his eyes as
the force of a blow ejected a near-soundless wheeze from him. His
mouth began to fill with the taste of what he was almost certain
was blood. A cacophony of shouts followed as darkness licked at
the edges of his blurred vision.

But before it all ended, Xerx was greeted by a new sensation,
precluded by a familiar piercing whine. A stabbing shock set his
every synapse on fire and flooded his muscles with the rigidity
that dwarfed the pain of his worst morning cramps to infinitesimal
levels. Its only saving grace had been its brevity before blessed
darkness claimed him.

FIFTEEN

Xerx's vision and hearing were clear enough to see what Artemis had been dangling in front of him when he was awake, as well as hear the words, "Sorry, but we had to amputate" which put him back into unconsciousness ... but not before he overheard the conversation.

"Dammit, Arty! That wasn't funny," Paige had said.

"I thought it was funny."

"Why did you even remove it?"

"Synaptic relays in the arm were fried beyond repair. He didn't need it anymore."

A sigh.

"You really are a sick little bitch."

Xerx had just enough time to be annoyed before he slipped away.

His second awakening was more pleasant. A sudden fear surged through him—quickly quelled once he turned his head to glance at his still-intact arms. He sighed with relief but filed away the memory of Artemis' prank for later revenge.

His wife knelt by his side, and Paige stood in the background. He felt the back of her hand caress his face and smiled, despite the stinging pain in his back.

"Did you really just take on a Raider with a meat cleaver?" she asked, her tone not so much one of anger as consternation.

"Better believe he did," Paige said before Xerx could answer. She lowered herself to one knee beside his wife. "Not too bright, but you did marry a man with balls."

"Well, at least I know I'm alive," Xerx said, realizing that his mouth felt like sandpaper and tasted like rusted metal. Still, he managed a weak chuckle. "Heaven can't be this condescending."

"Careful there," Paige said, placing a hand on his shoulder. "Nanos still aren't quite done patching up the bone fractures. Red-headed bastard did a number on you when he slammed you into that bulkhead. You're lucky he didn't rupture any organs."

"Who patched me up?" Xerx asked.

"Them." She gestured outside of Xerx's field of vision, into which Artemis stepped, joining the other two women. "Artemis is a capable field medic. Nemesis used her own nanos to repair you."

Xerx frowned. "I'm not going to be coughing up black stuff like her, am I?"

"No," Artemis said, pairing her response with a slightly dirty look. He knew that his question might have made him sound somewhat ungrateful, but he considered it a bit of retribution for her foul prank.

"Well, it's good to see they've got more skills than just shanking people and scaring them half to death with other people's amputated arms," Xerx remarked with a shrewd glance at Artemis' green eyes. Her sour look immediately transformed into a knowing, mischievous grin.

The bitch.

"You should be okay to stand," Neela said, "but we'll have to help you up."

"Walking will be a bit tricky at first," Paige added. "But, again, you should be okay." She then lifted herself on her haunches and reached out her hand as Neela followed suit. Xerx grasped their arms as they grasped his, and he curled his legs. Afterward, he pushed his way up, gritting his teeth against stiffness and a persistent, yet tolerable pain that shot across his back. He groaned at the initial complaint of newly repaired muscles and bone, staggering only once. Paige and his wife braced themselves, keeping him steady, and Xerx reached out his hand to balance himself against the bulkhead. A ghost of the buzzing recoil from the ion cannon's vicarious shock to his system stuttered through his somewhat unsteady limbs, but thankfully, the majority of the pain in his back had begun to fade.

Xerx's gaze settled upon the massive dent in the bulkhead down the corridor only several feet away. Brogan and Ike stood nearby, blood on their hands and clothes, likely from the conspicuously absent bodies of the Raiders. Maria and Miranda were nowhere to be found and neither were Salt and Pepper. Though, he could deduce where those two were now, if the situation was finally resolved.

"That dent looks just as painful as you probably feel, doesn't it?" Paige asked.

"Worse," Xerx said.

"Your heart stopped," Neela admitted. She spoke in a soft voice.

"What?"

"Big Red got hit with an ion cannon while holding you," Paige said, chuckling bemusedly. "What'd you think was going to happen? Don't worry; you're fine now. Arty guided Nemesis with precision, and they both did a sterling job."

"Well, she could've left me with less of a pain in my back," Xerx said cheekily.

"You're just stiff," Artemis said.

"Gotta agree with her there," Ike remarked, approaching with Brogan. "Their nanos are crazy effective. I saw Arty rebuild one of her arms from the shit in a waste reclamation unit once."

"That's both impressive and nauseating," Xerx said. "What about Salt and Pepper?"

"They're on the bridge with Var and Mobola," Neela said.

"Arty and Nemesis treated Salt's ears as well," Paige added. "He's doing fine now."

"Wait," Xerx said. "He was treated? How long was I out?"

"Only about an hour," Neela replied.

"Really now?" Xerx said, nonplussed. "I figured Salt would still be in the infirmary."

"He almost had to be," Brogan said on the edge of a laugh.

"He wasn't nearly as pliant as you, considering his experience with the blue-haired one," Neela explained. "Paige almost had Brogan restrain him. But he came around after he saw them work on you. His problem was much more easily fixed."

"And he's probably regretting that treatment if he's got to listen to Pip's prattling," Paige said, rolling her eyes. "Can you walk, chicken?"

Xerx nodded after taking a couple of steps forward. "Yeah. I'm good," he said. The pain was a slight annoyance but tolerable. He noticed the blood splatters and scoring marks on the floor and walls of the corridor and grimaced. "Guess our little guest couldn't kill those guys any neater?"

"You want it done neat or right?" Artemis said.

"Touché." Xerx made a self-deprecating smile. "Where are the tanks?"

"In the brig, looking after the big one," Neela said.

"He was the only one left alive," Paige said. "I had to stop Nemesis from offing him; I figured you wanted him alive with how you took him down. If not, we could still space him like we did with the bodies."

"I'm glad you left him alive," Xerx said. "Iriid's got a bounty on the heads of these malcontents. He's been hunting them down for years. He'll be glad to have one less out there."

"And we'll be sharing the bounty, right?" Paige asked expectantly. "He's valuable to me as well. I owe the Queen some favors, and I'm pretty sure she'll be happy to see one of these shits put on ice."

"Fair enough," Xerx said. "The bounty's pretty substantial, and I could use it with the future repair bill. I'll get in touch with Alexa, and we'll hammer it all out."

"Oh, by the way, I also thought you'd like to know that Nemesis went back to the observation deck," Paige said. "She left right as you woke up. She's volunteered to stay there until we get back to Siberna, so I doubt she'll be any trouble."

"Speaking of Siberna, how will we know where to contact this Four guy?" Xerx asked.

"Oh, don't worry," Paige said. "Knowing him, he'll contact you."

"Well, if that's the case, then those are two problems that just solved themselves," Xerx remarked. "I'll have Salt keep an eye on her until we get to Siberna. I still don't trust her, but I feel like I actually owe her one now. That's a weird-ass feeling."

"I'm sure you'll still be happy to be rid of her, right?" Paige asked.

"Immensely." Xerx nodded as he felt a new bounce in his step in spite of the niggling pain. "Now let's go to the bridge. It'll be nice to feel safe on my own ship again."

"Pip's done some improvements to the computer systems with Mobola," Neela mentioned as she took the lead. "You shouldn't run into the problems you had today ever again."

"I sure hope not," Xerx said. "That was more excitement than I needed."

"Can I go now?" Artemis said to Paige, who sighed.

"Yes, *now* you can go," she said to the shorter girl, who smiled and vanished around the nearby corner. "Sorry, she's been asking that since she and Nemesis stabilized you."

"Where's she going?" Xerx asked.

"To meet Maria," Paige said as Neela took the lead. "Those two have been joined at the hip ever since Maria proposed to her.

Before that, she used to hang out with Charlie, her promoter, in Pit Town. Haven't seen much of him lately though."

"Exchanging a surrogate brother for a surrogate wife?" Xerx said.

"Oh, there's nothing surrogate about it," Paige replied, "if Pip's spy recordings are to be believed."

Xerx wrinkled his nose. "Don't tell me she still does that shit."

"We all have our vices, love," Paige replied with a helpless shrug.

The rest of the trip to the bridge was blessedly without event. As they entered the scanner-laden corridor that led to the bridge, Paige tapped her comm. "Are we ready to finish this up, Pip?"

"Been ready for the last half-hour," Pip answered. "*Shadow Star*'s drive system is synced with the *Reckless*."

"What's she on about?" Xerx asked.

"We'll be bailing you out of the gravity well," Paige said, "at least until we can get that shield power balance rectified. You might want to get some specialists to look at that when you get to Siberna. I can recommend some really discreet ones."

The bridge door opened. A smile broke across Xerx's face as he was greeted by the sight of his crew at their places, as if they hadn't all just had a near brush with death over an hour before. Neela, who had been following silently, smiled as well, but for different reasons.

"It looks like you owe her big time," she said.

"Oh, I know it," Paige replied, fixing Xerx with a shrewd grin. "And don't think I won't collect on it."

"Then let's start with that drink I promised you," Xerx said, "but you deserve something top shelf. Nemesis ruined that, so we'll get it in Pit Town."

"Everything's green, Captain!" Pip shouted from her place beside Mobola, who bounced in her seat, startled at the diminutive tank's outburst. Paige glared at Pip, while Xerx, stepping onto the dais, noticed that Neela had chuckled at Mobola's reaction. "Ready to leave this shit storm on your command!"

Halfway to the top, he paused for a moment to lean over the railing. There was a hologram above the center of the bridge that displayed an image of the *Reckless* and *Shadow Star* connected ventrally by the umbilical that Paige and her crew had come across.

"Good job," Xerx said to Pip and Mobola. "Both of you." He then switched his gaze towards Salt, Pepper, and Var, who were hunched over their respective consoles. "And you guys too." He then smiled warmly at his wife. "And you as well, especially for not chewing me out after I woke up."

"Even though you would have deserved it," Neela replied with a puckered grin.

"In fact..." Reaching the dais platform, Xerx then raised his voice, giving Mobola the order to activate the ship-wide comm. "For both my crew and Paige's, dinner tomorrow is on me, at The Greasy Gear in Pit Town. We fill up 'til they kick us out of the place!"

SIXTEEN

Four had arranged a pick-up for Nemesis above the southern pole, where, as Pip had suggested, he waited aboard a previously cloaked Imperial Mallethead, which de-cloaked only long enough for Nemesis to be sent over through the umbilical. Four kept his constant poker face and taciturn nature, ignoring whatever questions Xerx attempted to press him with over the comm, but Nemesis, however, had been surprisingly forthcoming.

"I just want to know why you saved my life," Xerx said before the blue-haired girl stepped into the airlock, "after all you did to capture me."

"I wasn't ordered to kill you," Nemesis said. "And I was ordered to help you after you found me."

"So you've been in communication with Four?" Xerx said. "This whole time?"

"Yes. And even if my orders had been changed again, they would not have been to terminate. You'd be no good to us dead."

Xerx stared at her for nearly half a minute, his emotions oscillating between confusion and cold dread.

"You're a scary girl," he at last said. "But I guess it could've been worse."

"You thought I was sent by that Doctor?" Nemesis asked.

"How the hell did you know that?"

"We know more about you than you think," Nemesis said. "And quite frankly, I think she's scarier than I ever could be." She then waved to him—a casual and eerily friendly gesture, before stepping into the airlock. It sealed shut and she floated across the umbilical to Four's waiting ship.

Alexa, the pirate queen, had been thrilled over the news of the Raider malcontent's capture, and as the *Reckless* would still be in need of repairs and system checks, Xerx had agreed for Paige to make the transfer. The task of moving the big man from ship to ship, however, was, for a moment, something of a chore, as the now one-armed Raider certainly did not go quietly. Red had put up a valiant attempt at resistance for its brevity but was hardly a match for Maria and Brogan's combined obscene strength, or a well-placed, low-level shot from Maria's newly-acquired ion cannon. Cowed at last, he resigned himself to his fate. Good riddance.

Though he was thankful that the last of his problems had now been expunged from his ship, the work, however, was far from over. The pulsar had taken care of the bodies of the dead Raiders; still, there were bloodstains to tend to and a royal mess in the main hangar bay, to say nothing of the repairs in the masticated sections of the corridors, as well as the Grasshopper. Strangely, the damaged elevator that Nemesis had torn through during her thwarted attack was nowhere to be found. Considering how many times space had folded in garrison mode, Xerx doubted it ever would be.

Even with Paige's help, the grueling task of cleanup took the better part of the night. By the time it was all finished, sheer exhaustion had set in, which drove Xerx and his entire crew to sleep throughout the entire following day at their hangar while Paige and her crew rested aboard their respective ship. Gregor appeared to have taken his leave, and with the absence of the bodies left behind from the initial kerfuffle in the streets, Xerx surmised that pulling the right strings with the locals had been the old guy's repayment for their help.

In contrast to the prior night, their celebration at Pit Town's Greasy Gear that very next afternoon was long and raucous, though civil enough not to cause a fuss among the patrons outside of the rented private room. Even Var did not allow his prodigious capacity for booze to drive him to do anything foolish—something Xerx was grateful for, considering the time he snuck behind the counter and emptied the bartender's specialty stock. He'd spent the next month working it all back in the kitchen in lieu of equal time in the slam for one of the few things in Pit Town one could get arrested for. In fact, aside from a couple of broken dishes as any kind of grievance, the bill was perhaps the only misfortune of that night. Thankfully, Xerx's considerable GI Tournament winnings easily covered it, and with the added bonus of the bounty, he knew that he'd dodged a potentially problematic bullet with all the bedlam and destruction of the prior evening. Now, they could at last take it easy. Even Mobola seemed to have cut loose somewhat, as Neela had observed and drew Xerx's attention to with an amused grin. She had drunk a bit more than she probably ought to have, seeing how she'd fallen asleep on Pepper's shoulder in the middle of their own conversations with Pip.

Along with Neela, Xerx held back on any excess of food or drink, favoring instead, their own promised stress relief from their prior brush with death. With another round of hearty thanks to the now quite inebriated Paige and her crew, and the rest of their crew having turned in at their own lodgings in Pit Town, they absconded to the now-empty *Reckless*, parked alongside the *Shadow Star* at the nearby Siberna Prime Spaceport. Alone in their itinerant home, they chose the intimate privacy of their quarters to celebrate their survival in their own way.

Xerx awoke to his wife resting her head on his chest. She was breathing softly, but not quite asleep, he discovered, as she stirred with him. Her large eyes opened wide, without a hint of sleepiness as she gazed lovingly his way.

"Can't sleep either?" he asked.

"That's the drawback to all the sleep we had the prior night, I guess," Neela said with a sigh. She sat up and reclined against the headrest of their bed alcove.

"Yeah... all that cleanup. Fun times." Xerx shook his head ruefully, then smiled at the memory of Mobola and Pepper, her sound asleep while Pip prattled on, too into whatever schematic she was talking about to notice. "At least it's good to see that my two favorite people got closer after this. Nothing like a brush with death to make the heart grow fonder, eh?"

"You won't quit, will you?" Neela said, pursing her lips. "*Kipenzi...*"

"Hey, you're the one who pointed them out," Xerx said. "You're saying they're not good for each other?"

"Of course, I think they are," Neela said.

"Then let's just be happy that things are looking ... better," Xerx remarked with some thought. "Besides, it's better than contemplating the elephant in the room."

"The assassin?" Neela said.

Xerx nodded.

"But she saved your life."

"And she's just as likely to put a bullet in my head the next time," Xerx countered. He absently rubbed the pirate clan tattoo on his left shoulder. The double-ringed skull was a common sight on most Colony worlds, but it was a little-known fact that wearing the tattoo on the left shoulder, including the special blend of inks used in its creation, signaled a true pirate blood. He noticed Neela frowning. This was one of the fleeting times he wished he had taken her advice and had it removed.

"There aren't many people who know about my connections to the pirate clans or my family," Xerx mused aloud. He sat up and reluctantly turned to slip out of bed. "And there are more people in the Imperium who want to see the Clans wiped off the face of the universe than there are in the Alliance, so why would the Imperium come after just one?"

"They may know more about you than you realize," Neela warned. "You are the King's cousin, after all. He and Alexa have no heirs."

Silently, Xerx reached down and gathered up his clothes from the floor.

"You could have Iriid give you a dukedom somewhere on Rhoma if you wanted," Neela said.

"Not my style," Xerx said. "And you wouldn't like being my duchess either. Too many responsibilities, too many limitations."

"Ah, you know me well," his wife said, watching as he sat at the edge of the bed and began to pull his clothes back on. Xerx caught a glimpse of her leaning up on her elbow, eyes fixed on him. "Where are you going?"

"I promised Paige that drink," he explained as he slipped into his pants, pulled on his boots and shirt, and headed to the shelf at the far end of the room. "After all she did for us, the least I can do is be at the hangar on time." He selected the unopened bottle of Iconian whiskey, a wedding gift from Rico, Alexa's adopted father.

Neela gestured toward the bottle. "You're really are going all out," she remarked approvingly. "Should I be jealous?"

Xerx gave a knowing smile. "Well, you know as a pirate, my word is my bond and all that jazz." He removed two glasses from the cabinet below the shelf and returned to his wife to share a last kiss. "Keep the bed warm for me, will ya?"

"Very well, *kipenzi*," Neela said, lying back down and closing her eyes. "Just don't drink the whole bottle. That stuff is very hard to get."

"I was worried you'd get cheap on me," Paige said, once they had decimated the contents of the bottle by half.

"You ought to know me better," Xerx said defensively. "Besides, you guys go through Imperial territory all the time. On this side of the line, it's a little hard to come by, sometimes even for pirates. I figured you'd be able to tell the difference."

"It's not that easy to get your hands on near the border either." Paige took the bottle and poured herself another glass. "Mostly bootleg shit; makes a great change to have the good stuff."

"Yeah, this stuff's the real deal," Xerx replied. "It was about twenty years old before we got it." He thought back to the wily ship captain who gave Alexa away during the royal wedding on Rhoma to Iriid. Having been born in the Second Imperium, the man owned a supply of the stuff that would have made a small fortune for any smuggler.

"Lucky bastard," Xerx thought aloud.

"Beg pardon?"

"Sorry," Xerx said, shaking himself from his brief reverie. "It's not you. I was thinking about the one who gave the whiskey to me." He poured himself another glass and knocked it back. "Besides, after the shit you got me and my crew out of, you deserve the best."

"Yes, I believe I do," Paige said, without a hint of self-deprecation.

"We both stick our necks out in our respective lines of work," Xerx said. "So ... to balls of steel ... and big ships." He gestured to the quiescent behemoths of the *Reckless* and *Shadow Star* parked beside each other, and he offered the toast.

Paige tapped her glass against Xerx's. "Mine's bigger," she quipped with a cheeky grin.

Xerx snorted out a chuckle. "No arguments there."

Just then, Paige's eyes widened. She threw up a finger before touching her temple. She said nothing, but the concentration in her expression was telling enough. She'd had her comm setup hardwired into her nervous system and inner ear, and with how quickly she rose to her feet, setting down her half-finished glass, it was no doubt important.

"Sorry, but I have to take this," she murmured and slipped away toward the stairwell entrance behind them, out of earshot.

Xerx, deciding to take one last drink before calling it a night, poured another glass and imbibed it. As he finished shaking off the warm burn of the liquid caressing his throat, his own comm began its chirping summons.

Dammit, I told them I didn't want to be disturbed, he thought.

"Var, this had better not be you drunk calling again," he muttered as he reached into his coat pocket and removed the comm. Without looking at the sender, he accepted the call. The hologram flickered on, changing Xerx's sour expression to one of surprise.

He hadn't heard from Isibar in nearly a year, not since he'd visited for the GI finals. His cousin hadn't changed much at all: same brown hair tied in a topknot over chiseled features, though his eyes seemed a bit blearier than before.

"Didn't catch you at a bad time, did I?" Isibar asked.

"Nah, just recovering from a near-death experience and a huge-ass after-party," Xerx said.

"Business as usual, then?" Isibar said as Xerx felt a grin spread unbidden across his mouth.

"How's Cala and the kids?"

"Kids are all healthy, and Cala's pregnant."

"Again?"

"Hey, she begged me for another," Isibar said.

"So that makes, what, fourteen now?"

"Fifteen," Isibar corrected.

"Shit." No wonder he looked so blasted.

"It's not uncommon for humans and Felyans to have big families," Isibar said defensively. "But that's neither here nor there. Remember that favor I asked about?"

Xerx's grin fell completely from his face.

SIXTEEN

It couldn't be!

"After the shit-show mission to Icona?" Xerx said. "The one I chewed you out for taking?"

"You're not the only one who did," Isibar gave a telling nod over his shoulder. "I damn near got killed and not just by the Imperium." He half-grinned with a snort. "'Course it helped that Cala was pregnant with number eleven at the time, so she couldn't skin me alive that badly."

"But on the subject..." Xerx prompted.

"Ah, yes. On the subject ... I managed to find *her*."

I don't believe it, Xerx thought. After this whole calamity, and his apprehensions, as remote as they were ... *now* it was genuinely *her*?

"The Doctor? After all this time?"

"Absolutely," Isibar said. "She's slipperier than a centipede eel, but I got her this time. It's like she'd been laying low all these years in hopes that I'd give up. I wouldn't have even found her if I hadn't kept a record of all her aliases. She cycles through them on a five-year basis and adds new ones all the time. I lucked out. Found her name and DNA profile on a transit shuttle's roster from Zynj to Tophanavar."

"Tophanavar?" Xerx frowned. "That's on the edge of Felyan space, nowhere near here. I'd lose half the season just getting there."

"Ah, that's where you'd be wrong, cousin of mine!" Isibar then held up a flyer with the GI logo featured prominently on it, but it was written in Felyan glyphs that he could not make out through the holo's spotty resolution. "I just got wind of plans for a GI charity exhibition tourney there. Shouldn't be too hard to get your team added to the roster, right? And considering what she's done, both to mine and yours, I think Felyan territory is the perfect place to get our revenge, don't you?"

EPILOGUE

After having concluded her call, Paige, standing across the way, eyed Xerx chatting with the hologram of his cousin. Transmissions from An'Re'Hara were notoriously expensive, so it certainly was not just about catching up on life, at least not at this ungodly hour. And though she was not one for eavesdropping on friends, she nevertheless succumbed to curiosity, enhancing her hearing to catch snippets of his conversation once Maria had explained their newest contract.

Immediately, she wished she hadn't.

Shit, she thought grimly. Talk about a hellish coincidence. Of course, Xerx and his family would have a mutual, personal interest in this job. They had certainly never forgotten about this vendetta, even years later, and especially after the heartbreak and loss it had caused Xerx. She thought that Xerx had been full of shit for bringing it up just yesterday, but a day made all the difference. This job was almost certainly going to drum up some bad blood between them. But money was money.

Best to do it quickly, then, she thought, as with an apologetic glance toward her oblivious friend, she slipped down into the stairwell and hurried back to the *Shadow Star*.

AUTHOR BIO

Brandon Hill is a native of Louisiana and an avid and frequent reader of science fiction and fantasy, who began writing in the eleventh grade. Of himself, he says, "I am a 'classic nerd' and prolific writer who has had dreams of authorship since childhood. I sketch perhaps even more prolifically than I write and have drawings of just about every character my warped imagination has come up with. I hope to continue sharing these ideas, characters, and stories with others for years to come."

Terence Pegasus is a native of Northampton, Northamptonshire in the United Kingdom. Sharing the same love of science fiction and fantasy, he enjoys making kitbashes of various Warhammer 40K parts. Sharing the same love of sci-fi and fantasy and having forged a friendship with Brandon that began in the mid-90s with a mutual interest in 80s cartoons and sci-fi series, he and Brandon began their work on Wild Space Saga, eventually sharing his unique characters and integrating them into the story and providing his concept and technical work to its ever-expanding universe.

COME FOLLOW THE NORTHWEST
PASSAGE WITH US!

SUPPORT US ON PATREON!
www.patreon.com/WildSpaceSaga

WILD SPACE SAGA CONCEPT AND COMIC ART BY
TERENCE PEGASUS AND BRANDON HILL:
wildspacesaga.deviantart.com

ART BY BRANDON HILL:
brandonhill.deviantart.com

FOLLOW BRANDON HILL'S FACEBOOK PAGE AT
"AuthorBrandonHill"

Follow us on Twitter!
@DecKrash
@WildSpaceSaga

Be sure to check out Brandon Hill's other e-books, paperbacks,
and hardcover books, available on Amazon Kindle and Nook:

Wild Space Saga:
Wild Space Saga, Book 1: Between the Devil and the Dark
Tales of Wild Space, Book 1: Lifemates
Tales of Wild Space, Book 2: Rites of Passage

The War of Millennium Night: From Slate to Crimson
Double-Cross My Heart

The World of Five Nations:
The Hidden Meanings
Elven Roses

Virtual Law _Reunions_

COMING SOON

Wild Space Saga, Book 2: Wrath and Redemption

Bound by a vow of vengeance against the murderous and psychopathic Dr. Hayashibara, a fortuitous message from his cousin on her whereabouts takes Xerxes and his crew to the distant orbital colony of Tophanavar. A charity Gestalt tournament becomes the cover for his crew's investigation into the colony's seedy dives to find his prey, who has left a trail of occupied hospital beds in her wake. Meanwhile, Paige, the captain of the Shadow Star, is wracked with guilt when her newest job may well rob Xerxes of his long-desired quarry. But in the depths of the colony, all is not as it seems, and the cagey Doctor is a master of deception, leaving one of Xerxes' crewmates ill and the neophyte captain desperate for revenge. Relatives and old friends join in the fray, with the wily Pirate Queen Alexa performing her own unique investigations, revealing new, terrifying secrets of the Doctor's true plan. Will Xerx become consumed by his zeal, which may tear apart cherished relationships as he falls for the Doctor's deadly traps, or will he trust his friends to help him uncover the Doctor's true plans, possibly destroying a thriving colony?

More books from 4 Horsemen Publications

Horror, Thriller, & Suspense

Alan Berkshire
Jungle

Amanda Byrd
Trapped

Erika Lance
Jimmy
Illusions of Happiness
No Place for Happiness
I Hunt You

Maria DeVivo
Witch of the Black Circle
Witch of the Red Thorn

Mark Tarrant
The Death Riders
Howl of the Windigo
Guts and Garter Belts

Fantasy & SciFi

**Brandon Hill &
Terence Pegasus**
Between the Devil and the Dark

C.K. Westbrook
The Shooting
The Collision

D. Lambert
To Walk into the Sands
Rydan
Celebrant

Northlander
Esparan
King
Traitor
His Last Name

Ty Carlson
The Bench
The Favorite

Discover more at
4HorsemenPublications.com

145

9 781644 506387